PUFFIN BOOKS

BABE
PIG IN THE CITY
NOVELIZATION

Mr Hoggett, being a man of few words but a great listener, understood his wife perfectly. What's more, he agreed with her. In fact, in his quiet way the Farmer believed that the Pig could save the farm. After all, if a pig could become a sheepdog, many things were possible. Hoggett could only hope.

BABE

PIG IN THE CITY

Adapted by Justine Korman and Ron Fontes

Based on the motion picture screenplay written by
George Miller   Judy Morris   Mark Lamprell

Based on characters created by Dick King-Smith

PUFFIN BOOKS

PUFFIN BOOKS

Published by the Penguin Group
Penguin Books Ltd, 27 Wrights Lane, London w8 5tz, England
Penguin Putnam Inc., 375 Hudson Street, New York, New York 10014, USA
Penguin Books Australia Ltd, Ringwood, Victoria, Australia
Penguin Books Canada Ltd, 10 Alcorn Avenue, Toronto, Ontario, Canada m4v 3b2
Penguin Books (NZ) Ltd, Private Bag 102902, NSMC, Auckland, New Zealand

Penguin Books Ltd, Registered Offices: Harmondsworth, Middlesex, England

First published in the USA by Random House, Inc. 1998
Published in Puffin Books 1998
1 3 5 7 9 10 8 6 4 2

Puffin Film and TV Tie-in edition first published 1998

Set in 12/16pt Palatino
Typeset by Rowland Phototypesetting Ltd,
Bury St Edmunds, Suffolk
Printed in England by Clays Ltd, St Ives plc

British Library Cataloguing in Publication Data
A CIP catalogue record for this book is available from the British Library

ISBN 0-141-30195-3

Prologue

Do you remember, Dear Ones, the polite little pig who grew up to be a shepherd and a farmer's best friend?

That's right, Babe!

If you promise not to get your fingerprints on it, you may look at the huge brass trophy the two friends won together. The writing on it says:

NATIONAL SHEEPDOG TRIALS
GRAND CHAMPION
'PIG'
Owner
A. H. HOGGETT

Indeed, there's nothing true friendship cannot overcome. As you will soon see in this, the story of what happened when Babe and Farmer Hoggett returned to Hoggett Hollow.

Chapter 1

If only

The first hazard for a returning hero is fame. Those who once dismissed you as nothing more than a lousy pork chop now clamour just to be in your presence. The hero-worship can make you quite giddy!

And so it was to be with Babe. Babe sat on the back of a truck beside his human, Arthur Hoggett. Across his chest Babe wore a shiny Champion's sash. His eyes twinkled as townsfolk waved hats, handkerchiefs and bright balloons. Fluffy white thistle seeds floated across the green valley like a gentle ticker-tape parade. Babe could hardly believe all this fuss was for him and his human. All the people were cheering – and the animals, too!

A small boy was clutching his bulging

windcheater as he ran alongside the truck. Babe looked down and glimpsed three piglets snuggled in the boy's arms.

'Babe! Babe! Babe!' the piglets squealed.

A horse just beyond the fence whinnied, 'You've done us proud, Pig!'

Babe lifted his pink snout just a little higher.

Sheep trotted down from the grassy hilltops like woolly white clouds. 'Baaaabe! Baaaabe! Ba-a-a-be!' they bleated.

The little pig was starting to feel very big!

In the sky, an aeroplane completed a heart around the word 'PIG'. The fluffy letters floated in the blue sky. By the time the truck reached Hoggett Farm, the small pig was quite swollen with pride.

The Farmer's Wife came out to meet them as they approached the cottage. Babbling an endless stream of endearments, she folded the Farmer in her plump arms.

Meanwhile, the small pig was blinking in the glare of flashbulbs. Photographers swarmed around the truck like bees around a honey pot. Babe was a star!

The deeds of the Farmer and his remarkable Pig had become well known even in distant lands. Invitations came from all over the place: to open fairs, to give demonstrations of sheep-herding, even to meet the Queen! But Arthur Hoggett was

4

a quiet man. For him the greatest pleasure was to be found in honest work.

So, a few days later, the Farmer was glad to be back, doing what he did best, this time replacing the old water-pump. Hoggett hauled the new pump to the edge of the cobblestone well. He placed the heavy pump on a wooden platform, then climbed down into the well. From there he could lower the platform down to the bottom using a rope and pulley. This was the kind of work the Farmer liked to do; he felt much more comfortable doing this than shaking hands with strangers and smiling for cameras.

But Babe, his feet still not back on firm ground, somehow got it into his head that he could help. Fate turns on a moment, and the Pig was about to learn the meaning of those two cruel words, 'if only . . .'.

Babe leant over the side of the well in order to get a better look at what his human was doing. Right down at the very bottom, Farmer Hoggett held on to the rope and slowly began lowering the platform.

If only Babe hadn't been so careless . . .

As the Pig leant out, a block of stone gave way beneath his feet. The rock tumbled down past Hoggett and into the water.

SPLASH!

The Farmer looked up to see Babe falling forward, on to the platform!

If only the Pig and pump together hadn't weighed more than the Farmer . . .

Hoggett, still holding on to the rope, was suddenly jerked up into the air, like a puppet on a string!

If only the Farmer hadn't hit the platform as they passed . . .

THWACK!

Or jammed his fingers in the pulley at the top . . .

OUCH!

If only the Pig and the pump had not fallen off the platform at the bottom of the well. Now, suddenly, the Farmer was again heavier than the platform . . .

BANG! The Farmer smashed into the platform on his way down.

And if only the Farmer hadn't let go of the rope when he hit the bottom . . .

Dazed and bruised, the Farmer let the rope slip from his fingers. Babe looked up to see the platform hurtling towards them . . .

THUD! Right on top of his master's head.

'Boss!' Babe cried. 'BOSS!' His voice echoed up from the well that was not nearly as deep as his sorrow.

*

6

The next day, the living-room of the cosy cottage looked like a hospital. Farmer Hoggett was more bandage than man, swathed in a complicated set of casts and counter-weights.

The Farmer's Wife wrung her hands as she talked to the doctor. Concerned friends, both human and animal, surrounded the quiet Farmer in his hour of need.

Everyone glared as the guilty Pig made his way to his injured friend's side. The cat snarled. Mrs Hoggett's lips were pinched together in an angry frown. Babe could plainly tell what she was thinking. *If only the Pig had become roast pork as he was meant to, this would never have happened.*

Babe sat down by the side of his master's bed, his head bowed meekly. Slowly Farmer Hoggett raised his bandaged hand and began to scratch the Pig's head.

He doesn't hate me! Babe thought. His eyes shone with tears of joy and remorse. His human was so kind! Even after all the pain Babe had caused him, Hoggett was still his friend.

If there was ever a moment when the Pig wished that his words could be understood by humans, this was it. In a tiny voice, Babe oinked, 'S . . . sorry, Boss.'

And in the shadows of the room, three mice were

7

sitting and looking on. One of them began to sing an old French song that was bittersweet with regret. '*Je ne regrette rien*,' the tiny voice squeaked. 'I regret nothing.' But, of course, the little Pig regretted that he had ever been born.

Surely, Dear Ones, you have noticed that things have a way of going from bad to worse. So it was on Hoggett Farm.

Even before the Farmer's accident, the Farmer's Wife had been ceaselessly busy: bustling, baking, bottling and pickling. Now she found life even more challenging as she tried to take care of her husband's duties as well,

One of those duties was shearing the sheep.

'Sa-a-a-ve me!' bleated one victim of her clumsy clipping.

'Ta-a-ake pity!' another begged.

But the Farmer's Wife was determined to do her best. Her Arthur needed her. It wasn't his fault he'd trusted that ... Pig. But now that they were in this mess ...

Mrs Hoggett released the old sheep she'd been shearing and went after the next.

'How do I look, Fly?' the old sheep asked.

The sheepdog, who'd raised Babe as her own, was not as used to being polite as the Pig when it came to addressing sheep. What do you say to a sheep that looks as if it's been dancing with an electric lawnmower?

'Um . . . well, er . . .' Fly turned to her husband, Rex. The aged sheepdog who had taken so long to believe in Babe tried to ease the old sheep's embarrassment.

'Don't worry,' he said. 'The difference between a good haircut and a bad haircut is just a couple of weeks . . . h-h-aw.'

Just then Fly spotted something on the horizon and she growled. Mrs Hoggett stood up and wiped her hands on her apron. She peered across the farmyard at two dark figures holding briefcases.

Mrs Hoggett gasped as the men started walking towards her. With their pale faces and soulless eyes, they could be from only one place: the Bank! No natural disaster – flood, fire or hurricane – could destroy a farm faster than men from the Bank!

In a panic, Mrs Hoggett raced back to the cottage. 'Oh my gosh! Oh my gosh! Oh, Arthur, deary me!' she panted.

The injured farmer lifted his head from his pillow. He watched while his wife frantically sifted through a pile of papers on the table, her face pink with exertion.

Then her eyes twinkled in triumph. Mrs Hoggett had found the letter she was looking for. At a speed that defied comprehension, the Farmer's Wife read:

THE STATE OF EXCITEMENT
PROUDLY PRESENTS
THE GRANDADDY OF STATE FAIRS
MORE LIVESTOCK, MORE THRILL-RIDES
MORE PRIZES PLUS
THE WORLD'S LARGEST PUMPKIN!

Mrs Hoggett had no time for overgrown vegetables now! She skipped to the most important part: 'Guest appearance ... your pig ... sheepherding demonstration ... plane tickets ... connecting flights ... and a generous appearance fee!'

Mrs Hoggett turned to her husband. 'Jumping jam-'n'-jellies, Arthur! We might just be able to do it!' By *it*, this is what Mrs Hoggett meant: go to the fair, earn the appearance fee, and pay the men from the Bank whatever they needed to let the Hoggetts keep the farm.

Mr Hoggett, being a man of few words but a great listener, understood his wife perfectly. What's more, he agreed with her. In fact, in his quiet way the Farmer believed that the Pig could save the farm. After all, if a pig could become a sheepdog, many things were possible. Hoggett could only hope.

'Pig, Pig, Pig!' Mrs Hoggett stood in the middle of

the yard and called for Babe. Just looking at the barn made her worry about getting wisps of hay on her best coat. She brushed at it automatically.

'Pig!' Mrs Hoggett called again. 'Pig!'

In the field the cow, horse, goats, rooster, sheep, and the sheepdogs Fly and Rex all heard the Farmer's Wife calling.

Fly and Rex looked at each other, then they trotted to the barn where they knew Babe was hiding. The dogs blinked in the hay-and-manure-scented darkness, so different from the bright, fresh day outside. They padded up to a large pile of straw in a shadowy corner.

Fly barked, 'Come, dear, you're being called.'

'Who, me?' a quick voice answered. Straw was shuffled aside as Ferdinand, the skinny duck, emerged from the pile.

Ignoring the nervous duck, Fly spoke gently to the pile of straw. 'Babe, you're to go with the boss's wife.'

'He's not here,' Ferdinand said.

'Babe!' Rex barked. The old sheepdog was as firm as any father.

From under the straw Babe's tiny voice said, 'Babe's not here.'

Rex scratched a flea that had been with him for a long time. 'You can't undo what's happened, son, but you can make up for it,' the old dog said.

The straw wiggled. After a moment, Babe came out. 'You'll have to excuse me,' he said, 'but at the moment I'm feeling a little . . . you know . . . forlorn and haunted.'

'You can't leave!' Ferdinand quacked. 'I need you. You're my lucky pig!'

Fly barked firmly. 'Babe, the Boss is about to lose the farm. We'll all be sent away.'

The horse nodded gravely. 'And there's no telling where we'll end up. Not every human is as kind as ours.'

Babe felt very small. 'But what can *I* do?'

'Nothing!' Ferdinand quacked.

'You're a sheep-pig,' said Rex. 'A champion no less. Most likely they want you to herd sheep. Whatever it is . . . whatever is asked of you . . . I expect you to do your best.'

Babe nodded and took a few slow steps towards the door.

Ferdinand flapped his skinny wings. 'Don't do anything you don't want to do. Pigs have rights, you know!'

In front of the farmhouse, Mrs Hoggett shouted, 'PIG!' one last time. Then she turned to her husband, who was propped up in a wheelchair on the porch. 'Arthur, you call the wretched thing!'

Farmer Hoggett spoke in his quiet, gentle voice. 'Come, Pig.'

Babe felt torn. He looked back at Fly. 'I don't want to leave you, Mom.'

Fly licked Babe's snout. 'You won't be alone, dear. You'll be with the boss's wife.'

Babe nodded.

Ferdinand ranted, 'Oh, sure!' The boss's wife! Slice, slice. Chop, chop. You'll be in the company of a serial killer!'

Rex growled, and the duck stepped back.

'Don't take counsel of your fears, lad,' Rex barked.

A cow added, 'And never listen to the delirious drivel of a demented duck.'

Ferdinand flapped his wings furiously. 'I don't recall anybody asking for your opinion.'

While they were arguing, Babe continued to make his way slowly towards the barn door.

'Do you want to pee before you go?' Fly asked.

'No, thank you,' the Pig replied as he stepped out into the sunshine and . . .

. . . into the arms of Mrs Hoggett!

'Come now! Chop, chop!' the Farmer's Wife said as she carried Babe to the truck. Babe suddenly found himself inside, looking out at the farm through a dusty window.

Ferdinand quacked desperately to Fly. 'But I need this pig. He's my good-luck pig! Without him I'm dead, deceased, lifeless, extinct, a demised duck, a cooked canard!'

Babe looked longingly at Fly. 'Can you come with me?' he asked.

The kindly sheepdog shook her head. 'I wish I could, dear, but it's you they want.'

'Please . . .' Tears twinkled in the little Pig's eyes.

Fly leant in close. 'Stop it now. You're a brave boy and, more often than not in this uncertain world, fortune favours the brave.'

Meanwhile Mrs Hoggett was giving a few last-minute instructions to two of her friends who'd be caring for the Farmer while she was away. She tried not to think about the many things that might go wrong in her absence.

Finally, the Farmer's Wife snatched up her suit-case and hurried towards the truck. She was half-way there before she realized that she'd forgotten something very important. Mrs Hoggett turned and blew her husband a kiss.

'Catch, it, Arthur,' she called.

Arthur Hoggett snatched the kiss out of the air and placed it on his weathered cheek.

Mrs Hoggett continued on her way to the truck. But before she could get there, the man of few words spoke one. Her name.

'Esme . . .'

Mrs Hoggett knew what he was thinking.

'Don't worry, Heart,' she said. 'I'll guard him with my life.'

And so the little pig took his leave of all that was home to him. Once again he travelled between the green hills, reversing the journey he had taken on the day of his triumphant parade.

Once again the sheep bleated from the ridges as he rode by. But this time they were saying, 'Save the fa-a-arm, Ba-abe! Sa-a-ve the FA-A-ARM!'

Their bleats mingled with the gasps of an extremely out-of-shape duck chasing after the departing truck. Ferdinand tried to take off as he panted, 'Doom! Doom! No breath, no life. The light ... at the end of the tunnel ... recedes. Oxygen, oxygen!'

'Sa-a-ve the FA-A-ARM!'

Even as the sheep were bleating, two men from the Bank were putting up a sign that read:

MORTGAGE SALE

And so, followed by the doom-and-gloom duck, the Pig and the Farmer's Wife ventured into the larger world. The appearance fee would keep the Bank at bay until Farmer Hoggett was back on his feet. If luck was on their side, they might just make it.

What follows, Dear Ones, is an account of their calamitous adventures ... and how a kind and steady heart can mend a sorry world.

Chapter 2

Scram! This is not a farm!

VA-ROOM! The huge jumbo jet rumbled as its giant engines roared into life. In his little cage in the cargo hold, Babe tried to be brave. The little pig sang to himself in a soft, quavering voice, 'La, la, la . . . La, la, la . . .'

Babe took a deep breath and tried to sing louder, but the engines drowned out the Pig's song.

Inside the aeroplane, Mrs Hoggett watched the flight attendant as she went through the safety instructions. Bored passengers glared at the Farmer's Wife for wearing her life jacket and . . . *whoosh*! . . . inflating it right there in the cabin.

Outside, Ferdinand tapped on the window. But no one noticed the desperate duck. As the plane took off, Ferdinand was left, flapping, far behind. He flew as hard as his little wings would take him, but the plane grew smaller and smaller until it was just a tiny dot in the sky.

Then he heard a chorus of voices behind him. Ferdinand was soon overtaken by a flock of geese, swinging along and singing, '*Pardon me, boys. Is that the cat-that-chewed-your-new-shoes?*'

Ferdinand puffed to the nearest goose, 'See that . . . fat . . . featherless . . . flying thing?'

The goose nodded his long neck. Of course he could see the aeroplane.

'Know . . . where it's headed?' Ferdinand huffed.

The goose answered in song, '*Yeah, yeah. Follow us!*'

The cage containing Babe was unloaded and delivered by conveyor belt to a dimly lit cavern.

'Er, excuse me . . .' Babe said, his little snout pressed up against the bars of the cage. Babe was addressing the only other living creature in the huge room. A hyper-active beagle, wearing a jacket with the words DRUG DETECTION printed on it, was sniffing his way through the mountains of luggage, one suitcase at a time.

'Excuse me,' Babe tried again, 'but I was wondering . . .'

The dog just kept sniffing. 'Look, pal, I'm busy.'

'I-I seem to have lost my human,' Babe said. 'Sh . . . she's . . .'

17

'Hey! I'm working here! Earning a living, *comprenez*?' The beagle turned and for the first time saw who had been speaking. 'Whoa! Ain't you a weird-looking puppy!'

'I'm not a puppy,' Babe said. 'I am a sheep-pig. And my human is gone and I'm hungry and I'm supposed to save the Farm.'

'Yeah, yeah. That's truly tragic,' the dog barked gruffly. 'But you see that long line of stuff over here, and all those piles over there? Well, I gotta sniff every doggone one of them. Sniff, sniff, sniff. I'm a Sniffer, ya see? A fully qualified, triple-certified Sniffer.'

The beagle lifted his big wet nose for Babe to see. 'It's all in the hooter, the schnoz, the olfactory instrument,' he said. The beagle looked hard at Babe's snout with its wide, moist tip. 'You could be a sniffer with a schnoz like that.'

'That's very kind of you,' Babe said, 'but . . .'

'Hey! You got something against sniffing?' the beagle asked. 'Listen, Fido, it ain't as easy as it looks! It takes a lot of educatin'. Knowin' the smells, knowin' precisely what to sniff . . .'

'I didn't mean to offend . . .' Babe said.

'Hold on, I'm just getting to the good part!' the beagle said. 'When ya sniff the right smell, y'know what happens? Do ya? Do ya?' he asked excitedly.

Babe shook his head.

'You jump up and down and go berserk!' the beagle answered gleefully. 'Barkin' Beef-bones! You should see the humans come runnin'.'

'They do? Why?' Babe asked.

'Beats me, but I get big rewards.'

Babe was intrigued. 'Rewards?'

'Sure! My heart's desire! Watch this!' The beagle started barking. Right in Babe's face!

Customs officials hurried to see which bag was causing all the fuss. When they found out who the bag's owner was, they stared in surprise.

The customs officer shook his head. 'She could be my mom,' he said.

The officer's partner agreed. 'Yeah. Creepy, isn't it?'

Mrs Hoggett was quickly surrounded by a group of customs officers. The first approached her cautiously.

'Esme Cordelia Hoggett?' he asked.

'Oh thank heavens!' Mrs Hoggett said. She was glad to see the official. She had to find the Pig in time to make their connecting flight!

'Ma'am, we have the pig,' the officer said.

'Well, what are we waiting for?' said Mrs Hoggett. 'Come on! Chop, chop! If we miss Flight 115, we won't make the 4.15 shuttle. And if we miss the shuttle, we won't arrive on time for the fair. And if we miss the fair, we won't earn the appearance money. And if we don't have the money, the Bank won't take "Sorry, I missed the flight" for an answer . . .'

Mrs Hoggett was so busy chattering, she scarcely noticed that the officers were herding her into an interrogation room where Babe was sitting in the middle of a stainless-steel table beneath his own illuminated X-ray.

A female officer approached Mrs Hoggett. 'Esme Cordelia Hoggett, we have reason to believe that you may be carrying illegal substances on your person. As an Officer of the Drug Enforcement Agency, I am authorized by law to undertake certain procedures . . .'

Next Mrs Hoggett was examined more closely than a prize pig on market day. When it was over, of course it was proved beyond a shadow of a doubt that Esme Cordelia Hoggett was of virtuous character, but, sadly, by now the Farmer's Wife and Pig had missed their all-important connecting flight. And, to make matters worse, they were obliged to wait some days for the next flight home. They couldn't go onward and they couldn't go back. They were stranded at the airport.

Mrs Hoggett tried calling hotels. None would take pets!

'It's only a *little* pig,' she explained to the first hotel. The phone clicked. Mrs Hoggett tried again.

'Well, it's more of a dog, really.' Another hotel employee hung up. Mrs Hoggett tried yet again. 'But he's practically human!' she wailed.

No hotel, it seemed, would open its doors to the Farmer's Wife and Pig. Mrs Hoggett fell asleep on a bench, cradling Babe in her arms. The once-bustling airport was now deserted, except for the sleeping Farmer's Wife, her Pig, the night cleaner and the security guard.

'Move on, lady. No animals in the airport,' the guard said gruffly.

Mrs Hoggett yawned. 'You don't understand. We've nowhere to . . .'

The guard understood. He just didn't care. 'Scram!' he shouted. 'This is not a farm.'

Mrs Hoggett spent the rest of the night in the deserted airport avoiding the security guard. Towards dawn, the resourceful Farmer's Wife dreamed up a disguise, and the deception worked on many busy commuters. Without a second glance, they bustled past the plump woman cradling a large baby swaddled in her arms.

But, alas, the security guard was not so easily fooled. He tapped Mrs Hoggett on the shoulder. She looked up, her 'baby' snuggled against her shoulder. Babe's twinkly gaze was as innocent as a newborn's. But his long snout and floppy ears made for a very peculiar-looking infant.

The guard was not impressed by Mrs Hoggett's resourcefulness. He herded the Farmer's Wife and the Pig out into the noisy street.

Horns honked. Brakes squealed. Limousines swarmed the roads like busy beetles. The acrid smell of exhaust fumes filled the air.

Mrs Hoggett took a deep breath and got ready to set out into the chaos. But before she could do so, the night cleaner trotted up and handed Mrs Hoggett a slip of paper:

THE FLEALANDS HOTEL
349 RANDOM CANAL

'I didn't give you this,' he said.

Mrs Hoggett studied the round, pink face of the stranger and wondered what had provoked this unexpected act of kindness. Small, twinkly eyes blinked back at her with the loving look of a well-fed pig! Before she could thank him, the little man was lost in the flock of commuters.

Armed with only a destination, Mrs Hoggett set off. She clutched her battered suitcase and led her pig on a lead across a Grand Plaza, the likes of which the two had never seen before!

If you've lived all your life in the modern metropolis, you may no longer be impressed by the *zuzz* and the *buzz* and the *boom bang clang*. But imagine that you come from Hoggett Hollow, a

22

little green valley somewhere just to the left of the twentieth century . . .

Babe's trotters clicked on the pavement. His ears pricked up at the mixture of sounds. Dogs of every breed, from pampered pedigrees to the lowest alley mutts, moved to the street's snappy beat. Through a forest of legs, Babe saw police horses prance proudly by. They were nothing like the humble horse back on the Farm.

Before too long, the streets changed. The slip of paper led Mrs Hoggett towards the beach. The breezy promenade was bustling with every kind of human: muscle-men, motorcycle cops, bikers, rollerbladers, beachcombers and street vendors.

Finally, wide streets gave way to a crooked maze of narrow paths, canals and bridges. Mrs Hoggett had reached her goal. The Farmer's Wife stared from the piece of paper clutched in her fingers to the ramshackle four-storey building known as the Flealands Hotel.

Chapter 3

What kind of establishment do you think this is?

Mrs Hoggett knocked on the door. A face appeared behind a dusty pane of glass.

'I need a room for myself and . . . er . . . the . . . er . . . wee pig,' Mrs Hoggett said.

The door was flung open, and the Landlady stepped out. 'Are you crazy?' she shouted. 'Animals in here? What makes you think we take animals?'

'Oh . . . but . . .' Mrs Hoggett didn't know what to say.

'What kind of establishment do you think this is?' the Landlady clucked. 'Well, it isn't! Am I aware of the city codes and regulations? Yes! Do I support the new ordinances? Most definitely. Am I one to break to the law? Absolutely not!'

She slammed the door.

Mrs Hoggett knocked again. She didn't know what else to do.

'Are you hearing-impaired?' the Landlady squawked. 'Go away!'

Mrs Hoggett stood on the corner and looked around. Back in Hoggett Hollow, Esme always knew where she was going. But here . . .

'Oh . . . well . . . er . . . but . . . mmm . . . gosh . . . I . . . never . . . um . . . goodness . . . yes . . . deary me . . .' she muttered to herself as she walked past the side of the hotel.

'Psst!'

Mrs Hoggett turned and saw the Landlady waving to her.

'M-m-me?' Mrs Hoggett was totally confused.

The Landlady pulled her and Babe into a shadowy alley. 'How long do you want to stay?' the Landlady whispered.

'Er . . . two days,' Mrs Hoggett replied.

'Will an attic room do?' the Landlady asked. She led them to the hotel's back door.

Mrs Hoggett didn't know what to think. 'But I thought you said . . .'

'Oh that was just for the neighbours,' the Landlady said. 'Heartless meanies. Where do they expect these poor creatures to go?' The Landlady looked at Babe. 'Is he house-trained?'

'Oh, yes. Just like you and me,' Mrs Hoggett assured her.

The Landlady led them inside the Flealands Hotel. As they climbed a rickety flight of stairs, the eccentric woman rattled on. 'Do we provide meals? No. But is there a convenience store? Yes, two blocks south. And what is the golden rule? Never answer the front door. Why? It might be an inspector. Mind that step.'

On the first-floor landing, Babe glanced through a half-open door. From out of the darkness, someone was watching them!

On the next landing, Babe turned to see two dogs peeping out at him: Nigel, an English Bulldog, and Alan, a Neapolitan Mastiff. The dogs wore matching blankets with a tasteful, floral pattern.

A third dog, Flealick, shot out from between Nigel and Alan. Flealick's lame back legs were mounted on wheels. A chequered flag waved from the top of an aerial attached to the contraption.

Flealick sniffed Babe up and down. 'Canine ... er ... no. Don't tell me, I'll get it.'

Nigel, the Bulldog, whispered, 'Flealick, come back! We don't know where it's been. Do we, Alan?'

The Mastiff shook his massive black head. 'No, Nigel, we don't.'

Flealick kept sniffing. 'I need a clue. It's my nose.

26

Sinusitis!' The small dog sniffed even harder. 'Feline. Oh no, you're a cat!'

'Do I look like a cat?' Babe said.

Flealick squinted. 'Not sure. It's my eyes. Cataracts.' He sniffed again. 'If you're a cat, you've got no business on this floor. Get that? No felines on this floor!'

The inquisitive lame dog tried to follow Babe up the stairs, but his wheels got stuck. Flealick's efforts were making him wheeze.

'Good heavens, his heart condition!' Nigel fretted. 'He'll kill himself, won't he, Alan?'

'Yes, Nigel,' the Mastiff agreed.

As they neared the top floor, Babe heard a chorus of cats humming. The Landlady was still rattling on to Mrs Hoggett. 'Where's the payphone? In the foyer. Local calls only. Where does the little piggy stay at all times? In the room. Where does the dear little fella do his necessaries? In the kitty litter. Who empties it? You do.' She unlocked the door to the attic room. 'Any questions?'

'Oh, yes, my husband,' Mrs Hoggett replied. 'Where do I make a long-distance call?'

Mrs Hoggett stood a picture of Arthur on the bedside table. She picked up her purse and turned to Babe. 'Stay, Pig ... stay,' she said firmly.

Then she pulled the door shut behind her. Babe

jumped on to a chair to look out of the window. Building after building stretched as far as his eyes could see: skyscrapers, chimneystacks, statues, fountains, a great sweeping bridge, a towering clock. All shone in outline against the twinkling glow of the fantastic City.

As Babe looked out across this vast area, crammed with humans and other living creatures, he wondered when he would see his first sheep. Then the thought occurred to him: *maybe it wasn't sheep-herding. Maybe something else was required of him.* Whatever the case, in this place with its dark corners and endless possibilities, the Pig felt sure he would find a way to redeem himself.

Behind the thoughtful Pig, the door opened quietly. A tiny monkey scampered into the room and looked around with large, shiny eyes.

'Um . . . can I help you?' the Pig asked politely.

The tiny monkey, whose name was Tug, picked up the photograph of Farmer Hoggett and dropped it in Mrs Hoggett's battered suitcase. His reply sounded like nonsense to Babe, but Tug made perfect sense – if you knew how to talk backwards. 'Esaelp tnod pots em goind ym boj,' the monkey chattered. (*Please don't stop me doing my job.*)

'Beg your pardon?' Babe asked.

28

Instead of answering, Tug shut the suitcase and pushed it off the bed on to the floor.

'What are you doing?' Babe demanded.

The three little mice who had hitched a ride inside the suitcase scrambled out as Tug pulled the bag out through the door.

'Wait a minute!' Babe ran after the departing monkey.

Tug tossed the suitcase down to the next landing. THUMP! BUMP! Then he leapt after it.

'Hey!' Babe called after him. 'That belongs to the Boss's Wife!'

Tug was already on the next landing when Babe passed the room with the inquisitive lame dog in it. Flealick wheeled out of his room, snuffling and squinting. 'Whoa, whoa! If you're not a cat, stay 'n' chat,' he barked in a friendly tone.

Nigel and Alan watched from behind the safety of the door.

Babe did not stop in his pursuit of the suitcase. 'Sorry,' he called over his shoulder. 'Don't mean to be rude . . .'

Tug threw the suitcase down the stairs and rode on it like a surfboard as far as the next landing. Babe tore after him as Flealick called after them, 'Don't get out much nowadays. On account of Nige and Al and their nerves, and me on account of my hips. But don't be a stranger now!'

29

Babe was not listening. He was too busy keeping up with the monkey. Tug dragged the suitcase through a door, then slammed it shut in the Pig's face. BANG!

'Hey! Open up!' Babe called. 'Please, can you open this door?'

The door opened to reveal a creature even more unusual than the little monkey. Babe gasped at the sight of a heavily pregnant chimpanzee wearing a pretty dress.

'You got a problem, sweetie?' the chimp asked. Her name was Zootie.

Babe stared in utter confusion. This furry being was clearly an animal, yet she was dressed like a human! 'You ... um ... I ... er ...' the Pig stammered.

'Who is it, honey?' a deep voice inside the room asked. Babe looked past Zootie and saw her husband, Bob. The male chimp was also dressed like a human. He was lounging on a couch and did not take his eyes off the flickering images on the TV screen.

Zootie looked at Babe. 'It's ... er ... kind of a baldy, pinky-whitey thingy.' She blew her gum into a pink bubble.

'Show him in,' Bob said in a friendly tone.

Babe entered. 'I would like the bag back,' he said.

'Hey, Pinkness,' Bob said. He pointed at Tug.

'Look at the little guy. You wanna break his heart?'

Tug started to cry. 'Ili eb etutitsed no eht . . . steerts . . .' (*I'll be destitute on the streets.*)

'But . . . it doesn't belong to him,' Babe said.

Bob was unmoved. 'All I know is what I see. Tug comes in with the bag, just doing his job collecting stuff, and you barge in here accusicating and making demandments. I didn't see you with the bag. Who's to say it belongs to you?'

Babe had never heard such nonsense before. 'I'm definitely not leaving without that bag.'

A smaller chimp sporting a bow tie and check trousers took off his personal stereo earphones. This was Easy, Bob's younger brother. 'I don't think my big brother, Bob Boppaluba the Big Banana, has finished 'splaining how things work around here,' Easy said.

Babe faced all three chimpanzees. He took a firm tone with them, the way Fly addressed sheep. 'I have to warn you. I may be small, but I can be ferocious if provoked.'

The little Pig was surprised when the Chimps backed off. Then a deep voice rumbled behind him. 'And what have we here?'

Babe turned and saw a pair of polished shoes, topped by immaculate spats. Above the spats were the neat trousers and coat of a butler, a butler who happened to be a huge Orang-utan!

31

Bob answered the Orang-utan's question. 'We're in a negotiation with this naked pink individual.'

'Yeah, he's of foreign extraction, your Honour,' Zootie said earnestly, before blowing another bubble.

'Possibly even an alien,' Easy added.

The Orang-utan, whose name was Thelonius, thundered, 'You drooling imbeciles! This is an omnivorous mammal of the order Ungulata. An inconsequential species with no other purpose than to be eaten by humans. This lowly, handless, deeply unattractive mud-lover is a pig!'

Zootie had heard of pigs but she had never actually seen one. 'Oh, so that's kinda what they sorta look like.'

Babe did not appreciate the Orang-utan's tone. 'For your information, I'm a sheep-pig, and I've been sent to save the Farm. And, come to think of it, I should be saving the Farm right now! And . . . if you can't say anything nice, don't say anything at all!'

'Silence, you rude piece of pork!' Thelonius countered.

Bob liked the idea of food. 'So . . . will this little pink lunchness, you know, fulfil his destiny nutritionally speaking?'

'We shall see,' Thelonius replied.

Babe shifted nervously on his trotters. 'I feel very

uncomfortable with this conversation. I want my bag back, and I want it now. Please, get out of my way.'

To Babe's surprise, Thelonius and the chimps backed off! Babe turned and saw why. A human dressed in a stained and creased clown's costume had come into the room. The bright colours of the clown's suit contrasted unpleasantly with the sickly palour of his face. The clown, whose name was Fugly Floom, was gnawing a greasy drumstick and staring at the Pig.

Suddenly there came a loud noise from the hall. 'Uncle Fugly! Uncle Fugly!' the Landlady cried.

The clown quickly scooped up the Pig and dropped him in a trunk. Then he stepped out of the room.

The Landlady and a very worried Mrs Hoggett came running down the stairs. 'There's been a theft upstairs. Can you imagine?' the Landlady said.

Fugly Floom gathered up the dregs of his charm as his niece the Landlady introduced him to the Farmer's Wife. 'Esme Hoggett, Fugly Floom. Uncle Fugly, Esme Hoggett.'

'Perhaps we should call the police,' Mrs Hoggett suggested.

'No!' the Landlady cried. 'Have you forgotten? No police, no authorities! Heaven forbid. That would be the end of this place. Surely you understand?'

'Oh dear . . .' Mrs Hoggett fretted. 'I just phoned my Arthur to tell him at least his Pig was safe, and now I've gone and lost the blessed little thing.'

Inside Fugly's room, Babe popped his head out of the trunk. 'That's my human!' he squealed.

'Shh!' Thelonius hissed.

'But she . . .' Babe began.

Thelonius slammed the trunk lid shut.

Out on the landing, Mrs Hoggett was saying, 'The clothes . . . I don't care about the clothes. But the Pig? I can't go home without the Pig!'

Fugly Floom gesticulated and made drooling noises. Somehow his niece understood him. 'Approximately five minutes ago he saw something that looked like a pig exit this establishment. Where did it go? Left on Canal Street and then in the direction of the beach.'

The three mice peered over the banister and watched Mrs Hoggett hurry out of the Flealands Hotel.

'Listen!' one of them hissed.

Three pairs of ears heard a mysterious humming. They followed the sound to a door along the hall, where they found . . . hundreds of cats singing 'Three Blind Mice' in flawless harmony!

They all ran after the farmer's wife,
who cut off their tails with a carving knife . . .

Chilled to their whiskers, the mice ran, squeaking and eeking, back to the relative safety of the attic room.

Chapter 4

Chaos Theory

'Pig ... Pig ... PIG!' Mrs Hoggett cried as she searched the crowded promenade. All kinds of people were out that day, including two motor-cycle policemen!

'Pig, pig, pig, pig!' she called as she walked past them.

Pedestrians smirked, never imagining that the distressed woman might really be calling for a pig rather than shouting insults at officers of the law. If only searching for a pig in the city couldn't be misconstrued so easily ...

With a *vroom* of their engines, the policemen took off after Mrs Hoggett.

The good woman did not notice her pursuers. In fact, Mrs Hoggett was so intent on finding the Pig that she wandered off the beaten track and down a lonely back-street. If only the Farmer's Wife had been more wary of dark alleys.

'Pig, pig, pig...' Mrs Hoggett called out, attracting the attention of a street gang. One of its members was dancing on rollerblades. His large body moved in perfect time to the music.

Until he heard Mrs Hoggett. 'Hey what?' he asked her.

'I'm looking for my husband's Pig,' the Farmer's Wife explained.

'Yeah, right. What ya got in that bag?' the dancer demanded.

Mrs Hoggett froze. Then, not knowing what else to do, she began to dance! For a moment, the bizarre strategy worked. While the man stood, gaping in wonder, Mrs Hoggett ran!

But he grabbed her handbag just before she could get out of reach. Mrs Hoggett refused to let go of the bag. But nor would the dancer! The Farmer's Wife ran, dragging the man along on his blades. The rest of the gang followed.

When she reached the end of the alley, Mrs Hoggett swung the dancer directly into the path of the motorcycle police! The crashing cops caused a chain reaction: cyclists, skaters and skateboarders all collided in a chaotic screech of out-of-control wheels!

One skateboarder swerved and ran into a ladder. Two workmen were using that ladder to glue up a giant poster! The men fell, dragging half the poster down with them. And the glue came down, landing on top of Mrs Hoggett! *Glop!*

As if that was not bad enough, a beautiful rollerblader wearing nothing but a bikini swept past the Farmer's Wife with a *swoosh* of skates – and snatched her handbag!

As wet glue slowly slid all down her, Mrs Hoggett wondered how things could possibly get worse. Then sirens blared. Lights flashed. And a police sergeant came striding towards her. He flipped open the cover of his official notebook and gazed at the Farmer's Wife with a sceptical stare.

Dear Ones, let it not be said that Mrs Hoggett was alone in enjoying the excitement of the City. At that very moment, Babe was fidgeting behind a makeshift stage in a hospital ward, waiting to make his début!

Under the spotlight, Fugly Floom popped the cork of a giant papier-mâché champagne bottle. Huge soap bubbles drifted over the heads of giggling children, some wearing hospital gowns and others swathed in bandages.

Tug's tiny fingers poked at the bubbles. Thelonius held up a title-card bearing the phrase:

A CHAMPAGNE DINNER

Bob and Zootie were sitting at a candlelit table in front of a painted backdrop proclaiming:

THE FABULOUS FLOOMS
AND THEIR
AMAZING APES!

Babe was nervous! The blank eyes of a papier-mâché pig stared at him. This was even worse than waiting for the National Sheepdog Trials to begin!

Easy sat calmly on top of a magician's box. A veteran of many such shows, the young chimp assured the Pig, 'Just do what they told you. You'll be OK.'

'But . . . but . . .'

Suddenly, the Pig was rolling along! Fugly Floom was wheeling the magician's box on stage.

Easy sawed the 'pig' in half. Mechanical legs pumped furiously as Babe's bewildered head poked through a hole cut in the front of the box.

Thelonius held up another title-card:

SPECIALITY OF THE HOUSE

As Fugly split the box in two, a chain of pork sausages spilled out. The next title-card instructed:

LAUGHTER AND APPLAUSE

The audience obeyed.

Thelonius flipped over another card that said simply:

HAM

Easy reappeared with a silver-domed platter. Fugly placed the platter on the table and lifted the lid to reveal Babe's head!

Forgetting their various ailments, the children laughed. Fugly started to walk away from the table but Bob grabbed the clown by his trick suspenders. Fugly made it halfway across the stage before the suspenders *snapped* him back to the table.

Bob pointed to the restless Pig as Thelonius displayed the next card:

TOO RARE

Fugly replaced the silver dome and whisked away the platter. Babe peeped up through the hole in the table. 'How am I doing?' he asked.

Zootie pushed Babe's head back down out of sight. 'Not now, sweetie!' the pregnant chimp shushed the Pig. 'Not now!'

PARTING SHOT

The last title-card proclaimed as Fugly placed a ball in a small cannon.

Babe crept out from under the table. 'Excuse me,'

he asked Thelonius. 'When do I get my reward? You know . . . my heart's desire?'

'Get back under the table!' Thelonius commanded.

Fugly lit the fuse and aimed the cannon at the audience. The clown turned his back and put his fingers in his ears.

Easy turned the cannon to face Fugly. The audience giggled because they thought they knew what was coming.

Babe was trotting back to his place under the table when Fugly Floom turned back towards the cannon. The clown tripped over the Pig, and the large, flaming match in Fugly's hand set fire to the stage curtains!

Frightened by the flames, Zootie clambered up on to the sprinkler system. Bob followed, knocking over the scenery at the back of the stage in his haste. Props flew everywhere!

BOOM! The cannon exploded, shooting a bright spray of confetti and streamers over the whole scene! Set off by the smoke, the sprinkler system began to spray water over everything. Alarms blared! People and animals scattered in all directions.

Ever mindful of his honoured Human, Thelonius helped Fugly to his feet.

Frozen with fear, Babe watched as the papier-mâché pig's head tumbled towards him, then stopped just short of his snout!

Chapter 5

Fortune favours the brave . . . right?

Babe's gut was growling like an angry monster. For the past hour the patient Pig had watched while Fugly Floom stuffed his face in the kitchen of his Flealands Hotel room. Savaged wrappers and flattened cans lay among dirty plates and cutlery.

Babe had shut his eyes to cut off the terrible sight. But he could not close his ears to the sound of countless cans being opened, crinkly wrappers torn, whipped cream squirted, and mouthfuls hastily chewed as the clown gulped the food down.

Babe's sensitive snout had been teased by the smell of greasy hamburgers and piping-hot french fries. Capping the ravenous Pig's evening of torture was Fugly Floom's dessert. After the cakes, shakes, puddings and pies, Fugly still had an appetite for some chocolate.

The clown's adoring butler held a heart-shaped box of fine chocolates out to Fugly. Thelonius waited stiffly at attention while the clown tried to make up his mind whether to have a caramel or a truffle, before settling on both.

In seconds, the chocolates were just a smear. His meal concluded, the clown rose from the table with a resounding *burp*! Thelonius gently guided him into the other room, where the comfy couch waited.

While the loyal Orang-utan was in the living-room, the Chimps edged towards the chocolate box which Thelonius had left on the table. Bob's pink-tipped fingers reached towards the heart-shaped cardboard. They almost brushed the precious . . .

A hug, auburn-coloured paw whisked the box away from Bob. Thelonius put the lid carefully back on the box and carried it back to the living-room.

Meanwhile, the chimps were sifting through the pile of wrappers and sauce-smeared plates for any scrap of nourishment.

Babe trotted across the slippery kitchen floor to the table. 'Any food? Any leftovers?' he called up to the chimps eagerly. The sound of Babe's stomach rumbling was almost as loud as the words he spoke.

Easy glanced down and lobbed a jar down off the table. It rolled towards the desperately hungry Pig.

'Hey, what'd you do that for?' Bob asked.

Easy shrugged. 'I dunno. His belly's rumbling.'

Bob frowned. 'We look after our own first.'

'Listen to your big brother. He's, y'know ... ya big brother,' Zootie advised.

Babe did not hear the discussion. His head was deep inside the peanut-butter jar. But he just couldn't reach the last lick of the sweet, sticky goo.

Babe nudged the jar into the living-room, where it bumped against the couch. The hungry Pig jammed his face deeper into the jar that was now braced against the sofa leg.

Babe grunted with effort. He still couldn't reach the peanut butter! And now ... Babe tried to pull his head out of the jar. It was just as he feared: he was stuck!

Glancing up, Babe saw Thelonius gently remove Fugly Floom's shoes. The furry butler lifted the clown's feet on to a footstool and tucked a blanket lovingly around the man's shoulders.

Fugly Floom did not look good. Well, Dear Ones, Fugly had not looked anything like good for many years. But that night, following his feast, the clown looked even worse than usual.

Thelonius tenderly placed the chocolate box on the clown's chest. From the kitchen door the three chimps watched to find out what would be the fate of the chocolates.

Babe did not care what happened to the chocolates. For the first time in over an hour, the Pig forgot he was hungry. Babe had a peanut-butter jar stuck on his face!

If ever a Pig wished he had hands, this was the moment. He shook his snout up and down and from side to side. But the jar would not budge!

Babe's muffled grunts of frustration finally caught Theolonius's attention. The Orang-utan pulled the jar off Babe's head.

Babe's anger poured out. 'Nothing's happening like it's supposed to,' he said. 'I did everything that was asked of me. I got in the box. I put my head through the hole. I was charming. So where's my reward? You said I'd get a reward. Everyone's counting on me. 'Specially my Human. She'll be back very soon, so I better get my reward. Where's my . . .'

Thelonius rammed the jar back over Babe's snout! The Pig started to protest, then he heard a hiss.

'Psst!' Bob beckoned Babe into the kitchen. 'I

46

know where your reward is,' the chimp whispered.

'Oo doo?' Babe's voice sounded muffled, coming from inside the jar.

'Oodliedoodles of reward,' Bob promised. 'And I know exactly how to get it . . .'

Bob pointed to an open trapdoor in the ceiling. Easy started to giggle. Zootie gave him a quick nudge. Easy clamped his hand over his mouth.

''N' it'll 'elp saaae dde faarr?' Babe's garbled words came through the fog of breath clouding the jar.

'What? Save the *what*?' Bob demanded crossly.

'Saae dde faarr! Dde faaarrr!' Babe squealed.

'That thingy, you know . . .' Zootie said.

'Dde Faaar!' Babe grunted through the jar.

Bob didn't know or care what the Pig was talking about. 'Yeah, yeah, we know,' he said. 'And it's gonna happen. Truly-ruly. But if you wanna save the ''Fun'', you do exactly as I say, OK?'

Babe nodded. He had to save the Farm. And he had to get this jar off his head – not necessarily in that order!

Bob finally reached forward to the Pig's smeared prison. 'Now, I'm gonna take this off . . .'

Babe gasped in the fresh, peanut-free air! He hastened to express himself, 'Actually, it was save the f–'

'Uh-uh! Not a word.' Bob held up his hand and

nodded towards the living-room where Thelonius was watching TV while his beloved human was dozing in fits and starts.

The chimps built a tower made of rubbish in the corner of the cluttered kitchen. The pile of old newspapers, boxes and an ancient TV climbed towards the trapdoor.

'*I'd* go up, only I'm pregnant,' Zootie said.

'*I'd* go up, only I'm afraid of heights,' Easy explained.

'*I'd* go, only I'm collapsaphobic.' Bob wasn't sure what this meant, but he figured it sounded good enough to fool the Pig.

Babe craned his neck to stare at the distant opening: the hole looked awfully high up. Babe swallowed hard. His empty stomach rumbled aggressively. Babe recalled Fly's wisdom.

'Well, um, fortune favours the brave. Right? Have you heard that?' he asked.

Bob nodded impatiently. 'Indeed, my little Braveness. Absoposolutely.'

Bob gave the Pig a push towards the tower. Babe began a slow and perilous climb . . .

Ba-riiiing! In the living-room, Thelonius lifted the telephone receiver and listened.

'*I promised them a good show, a safe show, ya MORON! Whatever gave you the crazy idea of using a live pig? YA MATZOBALL!*'

48

The clown sat up groggily and groaned.

Thelonius held the phone away from the clown's ear, close enough for him to hear but not enough to cause severe pain.

'I always stuck by ya! When your own parents tossed you out of the act, I stuck by ya. When no other clown would touch you with a ten-foot pogo stick, I stuck by ya!'

Dwarfed by the telephone, the tiny, angry voice droned on.

'Henceforth, hereafter, I am no longer responsible for what I laughingly call your career. Floom, you're through, kaput, finished, finito!'

Fugly dropped the receiver into the nearby fish-bowl.

The plastic palace and few inches of water were not much, but they were all the feisty little fish had. 'Hey!' he shouted up at the thoughtless giants. 'I'm swimmin' here! I'M SWIMMIN' HERE!'

Thelonius picked the receiver out of the bowl, shook the water from it and put it back on its cradle. Then the huge ape bent down to the tiny fish. 'My apologies,' he whispered.

'I might come down now.' Babe's voice was almost as small as the tiny fish's. The Pig was balancing in mid-air on a chair that swayed like a seesaw.

'No, no! You're doing fine!' Bob called.

'To be perfectly honest, I'm s . . . s . . . stuck!' The Pig was rigid with fear.

'Don't look down!' Easy coached. 'Just don't look down!'

So, of course, Babe looked down. His trotters teeter-tottered! Babe held his breath and felt the world spinning around him. Suddenly, he found himself back at the edge of the well, nudging that fateful stone out of place. Bob's voice called Babe back from the brink. 'You're almost there.'

The brave little Pig tried to take heart. 'C-closer to the t-top than the b-bottom . . . huh?'

Ever so slowly, Babe inched his way towards the top of the tower. Who would have guessed that this plump, ungainly creature was capable of such grace? And yet, through sheer determination, Babe made it to the top!

The Pig held his breath until the swaying finally stopped. Only then did he dare to whisper, 'N-now what?'

Bob hesitated for a moment, letting the excitement build. 'Well . . .' He winked at Easy, who slipped out of the door. Then he said, 'This happens.' Unseen by Babe, Bob gave the swaying tower a shove! The tower swung wildly, first one way . . . then the other . . .

Babe's eyes widened! He held his breath and tried to keep his balance. But the pile of junk was

50

as doomed to fall as that stone loosened from the rim of the well. Babe tumbled, squealing, down the toppling tower of junk and out through an open window!

The plucky Pig ended up clinging to an awning hanging over the canal. Tug watched as Babe scrambled to keep his footing.

In the kitchen, the tower of junk hit the floor with a crash! Thelonius leapt up and stormed into the room.

'Well, it was like this . . .' Bob stammered. 'The naked pink individual comes in here intent on doing this stupid trick.'

'Yeah, stupid trick,' Zootie chimed in.

'Don't ask us to interpolate what's going on in that strange little head,' Bob said. 'But it strikes me as very destructive behaviour.'

Easy appeared in the kitchen door, one hand casually behind his back. 'Perhaps it's a cry for help,' he said.

'And where is the delinquent swine now?' Thelonius demanded.

Zootie didn't know what to say. 'Y'know. He's around . . . he's um . . .'

Outside the window, Babe's trotters slipped. The Pig squealed for help as he slipped down the awning and into the canal with a loud splash!

'. . . swimming,' Zootie concluded.

51

Bob shrugged. 'Go figure.'

Thelonius rubbed his forehead, then took a deep breath. The Orang-utan felt a headache coming on. 'I will not allow whatever mad mischief you have concocted here tonight to ruin another lovely evening. I am going back inside to attend to Himself. You are going to tidy up. This is a civilized household. Tranquillity will prevail.'

The chimps waited for Thelonius to go back into the living-room. Then Easy pulled his hands out from behind his back. His nimble, furry fingers were holding Fugly Floom's box of chocolates! The Chimps gave a hushed cheer and slapped hands in a high-five.

In the canal below, Babe came to the surface, spluttering. This was not good, clean, country water. The surface was scummed with a thin, oily slick. Chewing-gum wrappers, chunks of rubbish, and things too terrible to mention were floating in the sluggish current.

Babe did not like swimming, but Fly had taught him how, just in case. The little Pig dog-paddled through the cold water towards the hotel.

The tiny monkey who had watched his struggle opened the Flealands' front door to him.

The chimps' cheer was short-lived. In seconds, Thelonius was back in the kitchen. Zootie was holding a chocolate, about to pop it into her mouth. The Orang-utan reached out his hand.

'Please, just one, just one, one, one, one little oney . . .' Zootie begged.

But Thelonius took her chocolate, then he reached for Easy's.

'It's not fair!' Easy protested. 'Why take it all out on us?'

'We're being victimated against. He's an inhumaniac!' Bob added.

Thelonius's head throbbed. How could he explain Himself's mysterious ways to a mere chimp? 'Himself doesn't want you to suffer. He just wants you to learn restraint, discipline. He wants you to elevate yourselves!'

The Orang-utan reached for Bob's chocolate.

Suddenly, Bob tossed the sweet in his mouth and held the box behind his back!

The strong Orang-utan easily pulled Bob's arm to the front. But the hungry Chimp refused to surrender.

The arm-wrestle raged on as Babe stormed into the room, wet, shaking, huffing, puffing, and getting angrier by the minute.

'Hey! Hey! Anyone notice that I'm dripping wet over here? Anyone wonder why?' the Pig asked.

No one noticed, except Easy. 'I'd keep my trap

shut, if I were you,' the young chimp warned Babe as Thelonius finally forced Bob to drop the chocolate box.

'Why do you always side with the Human?' Zootie asked Thelonius.

'Yeah, you ashamed of what you are?' Easy put in.

Thelonius frowned. 'While we were hunched over, dragging our knuckles, Humans were creating all this. They are the supreme species. They make the world work.'

'Well, right now the supreme Himself couldn't tie his own shoes,' Bob said.

'Yeah, why is he always drooling?' Easy wondered.

'I'm sure he has his own good reasons,' the Orang-utan asserted.

Babe asked, 'Does he have a good reason for not giving me my reward?!'

'Does he have a good reason when he does this?' Bob demanded, as he let out a huge burp!

Zootie imitated Fugly's snore while Easy blew raspberries. The three chimps were soon busily indulging in the lowest form of monkey business. Bob even dared to take off his jacket!

'PUT YOUR CLOTHES BACK ON, YOU MINDLESS KNUCKLE-WALKER!' Thelonius thundered. 'You don't deserve his . . . benevolence!

54

He put the very clothes on our backs. He taught us to walk upright. He freed our hands for higher works!'

'BUT HE DIDN'T GIVE ME MY REWARD!' Babe squealed.

Thelonius went ape! He tossed the helpless Pig out of the window. With a loud splash!, Babe was back in the foul canal.

'Who's next?' the Orang-utan asked nastily.

By the time the exhausted Pig made his way back to the kitchen, the chimps were obediently cleaning up.

'Just tell me ... There is no reward, is there?' Babe asked.

Zootie looked up from mopping.

'Was there ever such a thing?' Babe asked.

Zootie said, 'Oh, little pink thingy. This is the city. As Bob always says ... What *do* you say, Bob?'

'It's all illusory,' he answered. 'It's ill and it's for losers.'

Babe didn't quite know what Bob meant, but it sounded sad and cynical.

'No guarantees, my little pork pie,' Zootie went on. 'It's a dog-eat-dog world, and there's not enough dog to go around. So you look after number whatsy. Get my drift?'

Babe thought for a moment, then he replied, 'I'm

55

not a pork pie.' The little Pig turned and walked slowly out through the door.

Zootie called after him, 'Whatever you say, cutey pie.'

Babe didn't know what he was any more. But he knew what he wasn't! 'I'm not a cutey pie. I'm not any kind of pie ... I'm a pig on a mission.'

The small, determined animal took refuge in his attic room. Babe stared out into the night. The city twinkled below like a huge fairy castle. The towers of tall apartment buildings glowed with the flickering lights of many TV sets, against which humans' silhouettes moved like shadow puppets. A mournful saxophone echoed from a roof. Seagulls soared and wheeled in currents high above floodlit skyscrapers.

It's tough if you're a pig alone in the city. With each small step you seem to slide a long way back. It leaves you feeling empty. And who do you turn to? Where was the Boss's Wife?

Babe thought it might help if he could recall Fly and Rex and their steadfast words. And he tried really hard. But the little Pig could barely even remember the face of his beloved Boss. The Farm was fading ... it had become just a comforting dream ... an echo ...

The three mice crooned a tune made famous by Elvis, the immortal King of Rock'n'Roll:

56

'Are you lonesome tonight?
Do you miss me tonight?
Are you sorry we drifted apart?'

Suddenly the night exploded with colour! Babe blinked at the wondrous display of fireworks. Never, except perhaps for a delicious plateful of Mrs Hoggett's cornbread stuffing, had he ever seen a more beautiful sight.

The next morning, Babe woke to loud thumps and voices coming from downstairs. He went out on to the landing and saw ambulancemen carrying Fugly Floom out of his room. The clown's face was covered by an oxygen mask, a tube linked a bottle full of colourless liquid and the clown's limp arm, and a heart monitor beeped at irregular intervals.

The Landlady was holding her Uncle's hand. She looked very worried.

The hotel, usually so alive with miaowing, woofing and other animal sounds, was eerily silent. At the first sight of strangers, the residents had all vanished.

The Landlady stopped at the door to throw a coat over her nightgown. Thelonius stepped out of the shadows, and the Landlady paused to gaze into the Orang-utan's frightened eyes. Then she looked away quickly.

When the front door closed behind the Landlady, the other animals emerged from hiding. To everyone's surprise, Thelonius suddenly made his way up the stairs, swinging from balcony to balcony, once more the powerful trapeze artist of the jungle.

The Orang-utan headed towards Babe! The startled pig stepped away but the brooding beast swung right past him, to land in the tower window above the hotel attic.

The ambulance siren wailed as the vehicle set off for the hospital. Thelonius's huge shoulders drooped.

Babe did not know what to do. Easy swung up to the old ape. 'Are we OK, Thelonius?'

The Orang-utan answered in a hoarse whisper. 'I couldn't wake him. I tried, but he wouldn't wake up.'

'He'll be back,' Easy said. 'Himself always comes back.'

Thelonius looked away. Babe went back to his room and crawled under the bed.

Perhaps, Dear Ones, you have forgotten Ferdinand. The demented duck had not given up on his quest. The frantic fowl had tried every trick up his feathers to reach the bustling metropolis and find his lucky pig!

The journey had not been easy. After flapping

his heart out with the singing, swinging geese, Ferdinand had hitched a ride with a sympathetic pelican.

The bird, unfortunately, dropped the duck among the targets of a busy shooting range, where Ferdinand's goose was very nearly cooked!

The sound of gunshots still ringing in his ears, the exhausted duck sheltered in the arms of a stone angel on the top of a gothic church. Ferdinand called out feebly with the last of his strength, 'Pig ... p-pig ...'

Chapter 6

A murderous heart

By that night, the only voice Babe could hear was the insistent moan of his grumbling stomach . . .

RRrgghh . . . rrrrgghhh . . . ooooff . . .

Babe's belly made such a fuss, he began to believe it was talking to him. The rumble became words: '*Foooood . . . foooood . . . ooh food!*'

Then Babe heard another voice. Bob said, 'Food. Anybody got any good?'

Babe looked down through the banisters. He saw Bob calling up from the ground floor. 'Hey, dogs! You got any edibles? Any nibbly-dibblies?'

Flealick appeared on the dogs' landing. 'We got a carpet with some nice spaghetti stains.'

'But we can't keep licking the carpet, can we, Alan?' Nigel the Bulldog fretted.

'No, Nigel,' the Mastiff agreed.

'Hey, cats! Cats! Got any food?' Bob yelled.

Four cats opened a door near Babe. They each sang in turn, then together in harmony, like a barbershop quartet. 'No, no, no, no. We have no food.'

Zootie looked at Bob. Her husband nodded. 'Well then, I'm gonna get proactivated. I know where there's food-a-plentiful.'

Zootie was alarmed. 'We're going outside without a human? Could be sorta dangerous in a lethally kinda way.'

'We'll stick to the shadows, honey. It's coolness,' Bob assured her.

From the attic landing, Babe watched the chimps leave. Thelonius sat, slumped in the tower window, as still as a stone gargoyle.

Babe could not stay still. He had to eat! Now!

The chimps crept along between the street lights beside the canal like the spies Bob watched on TV. Their reflections floated on the smooth blackness of the quiet water.

Bob froze, suddenly sensing danger. The chimps slunk into the shadows and listened intently.

Clomp clomp clomp! The odd noise grew louder.

Then Babe appeared under the street light. His trotters clomped, then stopped.

'Hey, get out of the light!' Bob cautioned him.

'Where's the f-food?' Babe asked.

'Shh!' Bob and Zootie hissed in unison.

'I'll do anything,' Babe volunteered.

Bob looked around the deserted street and said, 'Keep your voice down.'

'Really, anything. I have to eat!' Babe whispered urgently.

Easy was sceptical. 'You don't even have any hands. What can you do?'

'What can I do? I can ... I can do lots,' Babe babbled. It was hard to think over the noisy voices in his tummy.

The chimps moved on.

Clomp, clomp, clomp, Babe trotted after them. 'Er ... sheep! I can herd sheep!' he exclaimed.

Zootie shook her head. 'Go home, sweetie. You're making a spectacle of yourself.'

Then suddenly Bob had an idea. 'Wait a momentum. Ya know what, honey? I'm thinking I might have some of those sheep for him to herd.'

'You do?' Zootie was confused.

'Uh-huh. I'll show ya,' Bob said.

Soon, the animals came to the corner shop two streets away from the hotel. Neon signs buzzed brightly in the darkness.

Babe followed the chimps behind the shop. Security bars and warning signs decorated a chain-link fence that was topped with gleaming barbed wire.

Bob stretched open a small hole in the fence. 'They're in there,' he told Babe.

'What kind? Border Leicester or Scottish Black-face?' Babe could handle either type of sheep, but a good shepherd liked to plan these things.

Bob replied, 'Bull Terrier and Dobermann pinscher. Very exotic breeds.'

Babe had never heard of those breeds of sheep. But Rex had told him to do his best, whatever was asked of him. So the little Pig started through the shadowy hole. Then he stopped and looked up. 'Where do you want me to herd them?' he asked.

Bob answered, 'That's up to you. Just keep them occupied 'til we get the necessaries.'

'Okey-dokey!' Babe agreed. He wriggled through the fence. The polite Pig peered into the darkness and called, 'Hello ... hello? Anybody home?'

The answer was a long, low, spine-tingling *snarl*.

Babe shuddered. 'Um ... anybody else?'

A creature of pure menace hulked out of the shadows. The Dobermann spoke through clenched jaws. 'You must have a thin grasp on reality. Unless you're suicidal,' he said.

'I'm looking for some sheep,' Babe explained.

If the Dobermann's growl had been menacing, the sound that next issued from the darkness was totally terrifying!

The Dobermann shrugged his muscular shoulders. 'I warned ya . . .'

Raargh! A beast whose every atom was dedicated to death and destruction came charging straight at Babe!

Just before he turned and ran, the little Pig identified the blur of hatred as a Bull Terrier. This, of course, was not a sheep, but a breed of dog renowned for its ferocity. Once the powerful jaws of a Bull Terrier close on you . . .

Babe did not want to find out whether the horror stories were true. He bolted, and the beast's jaws snapped in the air, inches from Babe's plump rump!

Snap! The Bull Terrier's chain yanked taut. Both dogs were chained to a single stake in the ground.

Babe was already through the fence when he realized what had happened. He turned and poked his head back through the hole. 'What's wrong with you? I was just trying to have a civil conversation.'

The Bull Terrier strained at the chain with such fury that he started to pull the stake out of the ground.

Oblivious to the danger, Babe continued. 'Hasn't anyone ever taught you any manners?'

The Bull Terrier lunged. The stake popped right out of the ground!

64

Babe ran for his life.

The Bull Terrier crashed through the fence, dragging the Dobermann behind him.

Babe's little trotters skittered on the pavement. He wanted to run like the wind, or at least a race-horse. But he was just a pig! At every step, the dogs loomed closer!

Babe went squealing around the corner, doomed as a turkey at Christmas-time. But the dogs were divided over whether to take the corner close or wide and they wound up on either side of a lamp-post. Their chains looped around the street light's base.

Once again, Fate had spared the small Pig.

The Bull Terrier refused to quit! He tugged so hard that the Dobermann had to walk backwards. The big dog pulled free of his collar. The Bull Terrier, dragging chain, stake and his partner's empty collar, kept up his pursuit of the Pig.

Babe ran madly for the sanctuary of the Flealands Hotel. He scratched at the door and squealed, 'It's me. It's me. Please . . . somebody . . .'

Babe glanced over his shoulder. The Bull Terrier's jaws were hanging open. Strands of saliva hung from the large, terrible teeth.

'Let me in!' Babe begged.

Thelonius, still slumped in the window, lifted his head. Tug listened.

Babe pleaded, 'Le-e-et meeee iiinn!'

The Bull Terrier pounced! Babe dived, just in front of those jaws. Tug opened the door in time to see the crazed canine chase Babe around the corner. The little monkey quickly shut the door again.

On the far side of the canal, a suspicious neighbour opened her door and stared at the now-empty street. Her husband called from inside, 'Darling, don't get yourself into a state.'

'It's not my imagination. Something is going on in that house!' the woman declared with shrill conviction.

Her husband tried another approach. 'Hortense, you're missing the aria.'

Babe feared that he was about to witness his own finale. Having narrowly escaped the Bull Terrier, the Pig found himself snout-to-nose with the Dobermann!

The Pig veered wildly down an alley, but he soon found himself in an ominous place: sinister creatures stepped out from the shadows. These dogs and cats scratched out a bitter living on the streets. They slept in discarded boxes that were clustered into a miserable metropolis known as Cardboard City.

Babe ran past them, turned and spotted a junkyard: a vast landscape of old TVs, conked-out computers, and other casualties of throw-away society were piled high in endless rows.

Babe bolted along one of the narrow rows between the piles of junk. The Bull Terrier followed him, but the Dobermann ducked down a different row, hoping to set up another ambush.

At the end of the lane, the dogs found each other, but no Pig! They stared at each other in surprise. All they could hear was the sound of their own panting.

'Stop!' the Bull Terrier commanded.

'Stop what?!' the Dobermann asked.

'Stop breathing!!' the Bull Terrier said crossly.

Both dogs held their breath. Pant ... pant ... pant. Someone was still panting!

The dogs looked up and saw the breathless Babe, perched on a box, just above head height. The chase was on again!

Babe's trotters scrambled for a footing on a stack of plastic pipes. The slippery tubes rolled down on top of the dogs. But that did not stop them!

Babe balanced precariously on the summit of a mountain of clattering aluminium cans. With the same sickening certainty he'd felt when the tower to the trapdoor in the hotel kitchen had collapsed, Babe knew he was going to fall.

Ker-ash! Clatter! The cans sounded like metal surf smashing on steel rocks. The little Pig slid, out of control. He landed head first in one of the big plastic pipes! The sides were tight, but his own momentum took him towards the far end of the pipe.

Without a second's thought, the Bull Terrier dived in after Babe – and promptly got stuck! His stubby legs thrashed out of one end of the pipe; Babe's desperate head and frantic forelegs poked out of the other.

Homeless animals emerged from the shadows to gape at the amazing sight.

'Pig-dog! Pig-dog! Hot-diggety-blubbery-cat custard!' shouted one dog.

The Bull Terrier's flailing chain caught on a stack of tyres. The weight of the tyres tugged the dog out of the pipe. Meanwhile Babe staggered on, still stuck!

Then the Dobermann grabbed the pipe's other end and shook it so hard that Babe popped free!

But just at that moment, the pile of tyres finally came down, toppling everything in its path. Babe looked up to see himself about to be covered by a tidal wave of junk!

The Pig tried to outrun the junk, but it was gaining on him! Two terrified cats, also similarly doomed, ducked through a small hole under the fence. Babe threw himself after them.

Crash! The wave of junk smashed into the fence. Babe squeezed out on the other side, free!

But the persistent Bull Terrier and the deadly Dobermann simply scaled the junk pile and jumped over the fence to get back on Babe's tail.

The Pig's little eyes searched for a possible means of salvation. Babe shot through a gate that was propped open by a rusty old lawnmower.

The Bull Terrier chased Babe across someone's yard. The dog's chain got caught in the lawn-mower, and he simply dragged the clanking machine after him!

Babe ran past some garden chairs, then splashed through a paddling pool and into a tent, which promptly collapsed on him. Babe blindly thrashed his way through a wall of bushes, scattering fra-grant flowers everywhere.

Lights snapped on in a nearby house. A man in pyjamas rushed out in time to see the Bull Terrier and the Dobermann tearing a large doll apart.

'Mama! Mama!' the doll cried.

The man turned the garden hose on and blasted the dogs with cold water. The Bull Terrier turned on the man, who wisely ran inside! The hose thrashed around like a mad serpent, gushing water.

The Bull Terrier looked around in frustration. The only target its small, dark eyes could see was the Dobermann. He attacked!

'Hey! Ow! It's *me*!' the Dobermann protested.

The Bull Terrier was beyond reason. 'Massacre
... slaughter ...' the mad dog mumbled.

'I'm your pal. Your only pal, doggone it ...' the
Dobermann tried to reason with the Bull Terrier.

'... carnage ... *war*!' The Bull Terrier ground his
mighty teeth.

The Doberman took to his heels!

The Bull Terrier's eyes had turned into pits of
pure evil. His entire brain was given over to a
single terrible urge, leaving room only for a single
word: 'ANNIHILATION!'

A walking tent wandered into the park next
door. The strange, ghostlike creature zig-zagged
past a summerhouse, where the three chimps were
perched like gargoyles.

Their raid on the corner ship had not been a
complete failure: the chimps had managed to grab
a few chocolates and a large jar of jellybeans.

Easy climbed down the wall of the summerhouse
and grabbed a side end of the tent. The flap lifted,
and there was Babe!

Just then the Bull Terrier came thundering towards them, still dragging the lawnmower behind
him. Easy leapt easily back up on to the roof of
the summerhouse. He looked down, wondering
whether he should help the hapless Pig.

Easy shrugged at Bob. 'Why get involved, right?'

As the Bull Terrier closed in on his prey, Babe

70

tried to scramble up the side of the summerhouse. But there was no way he could succeed. Babe had no choice but to run!

An audience of homeless animals gathered to watch the Pig try to outrun the relentless Bull Terrier. Appropriately dramatic opera music blasted from the suspicious neighbour's house, as the tragic hero's trotters brought him back to the bridge in front of the hotel.

Thelonius stepped out on to the balcony of the Flealands Hotel to watch as the Bull Terrier chased Babe over the bridge. The terrible teeth scratched the Pig's rump in a first taste of blood!

But the lawnmower, still being towed along, knocked over a newspaper stand, and this gave the Pig a moment to contemplate his imminent destruction. Time slowed down for Babe. Each agonizing step, each deeply drawn breath had a kind of horrible awareness.

Something broke through the terror ... the flickerings ... the fragments of his short life ... the random events that delivered him to this ... his final moment.

The little Pig simply could not go on.

As terror gave way to exhaustion, and exhaustion to resignation, Babe turned to his attacker. His eyes filled with one simple question ... Why?

There was no answer, only action. The Bull

71

Terrier brought Babe down. The noise of a jumbo jet flying loudly past overhead drowned out our hero's squeals.

The spectators shuddered in the safety of the shadows. 'Shouldn't somebody do something?' a pink poodle with a faint Southern accent wondered.

'Not our business,' the itchy dog beside her barked.

The chimps watched from the summerhouse in the park. Nigel and Alan, along with other Flea-lands residents, peeped out from behind the hotel's faded curtains.

Nigel shook his large, tan-coloured head. 'This is what happens on the outside, Alan.'

The Mastiff added sadly, 'It's the times, Nigel.'

Flealick could not reach the windowsill. His chequered flag whipped back and forth. 'What's hap-hap-happening?!' he demanded.

Nigel could not bring himself to describe the horror. The Bull Terrier tossed Babe in the air as easily as he had the crying doll. But, as luck would have it, those terrible teeth did not pierce Babe's throat – they merely cut through his leather collar! The collar broke, and Babe went tumbling into the canal once again! *Ker-splash!*

Without hesitation, the Bull Terrier launched himself out over the sluggish water. Dear Ones, it

72

is often said that he who lives by the sword, dies by the sword. Anyone who dedicates his life to destruction will himself be destroyed.

So it was with the Bull Terrier. His launch into the air was cut short by the lawnmower, still being dragged in the mad dog's wake. The mower hooked around the fallen newspaper stand. Once again, the chain was pulled taut!

This time, the Bull Terrier found himself in a most unusual predicament: his hind legs were tangled up in the chain and the dog himself dangled upside down. The cold canal water crept past, just below his nose. Did this dire situation lessen his desire for destruction? Did the dog regret the cruel chase?

No! The Bull Terrier hung, swinging above the oil-scummed water, trussed up like a Sunday chicken, still boiling with hatred. Since the bound canine could not see anyone else to attack, he barked and strained at his own reflection in the brackish brine.

The chain slipped! The Bull Terrier's nose skimmed the cool water. Panic gripped his heart. The chase had turned on him: now the killer was fighting for his life!

The Bull Terrier's struggles only caused the chain to slip further! The mower broke free of the newspaper stand and the dog dropped, still dangling, still tangled, but now with his head fully under the icy, stagnant water!

Babe shook himself dry. A short swim through the greasy water had brought him to the embankment in front of the hotel. The Pig looked back to see . . .

The Bull Terrier was drowning!

Thelonius, Tug, the chimps and the other Flealands residents, the homeless animals and Babe, all watched the Bull Terrier's powerful legs kick and thrash. The scummy water around his terrible snout churned.

He wanted to live! How could *he* be dying? But he was. His legs grew weaker. The great muscles, deprived of vital oxygen, could no longer move.

The show was over. The homeless animals turned to return to their cardboard shacks. Nigel and Alan stepped away from the window. Thelonius turned his broad back on the canal.

Then they all heard a *splash*!

Babe was swimming towards a small boat that was tethered near by. The Pig managed to free the boat and, dog-paddling, pushed the craft towards the Bull Terrier.

The show was *not* over. The animal audience returned. Thelonius stared in disbelief as Babe pushed the boat under his attacker. The chimps gasped as the dangling dog's body twitched with life, the forelegs scrambling for a footing.

The homeless animals were amazed when the Bull Terrier lifted his head out of the water, choking, coughing, gulping in air. He was alive! But the dog was still tangled up in the chain.

The bystanders heard Babe cry, 'Please! Someone! Give us a hand!'

A tiny monkey climbed down to the chain. Tug looked at Babe and shrugged. *'Dnah taht ro dnah siht?'* he asked. (*This hand or that hand?*)

The silly monkey giggled at his own joke, but he quickly unhooked the Bull Terrier's chain from his collar. Babe made for the shore as the dog wriggled free of the chain.

Babe collapsed on dry ground. The exhausted Pig was soon surrounded by homeless animals eager to make his acquaintance. Babe was a hero once more!

The pink poodle sidled up to the Pig. Her once-glamorous curls were slightly matted, the proud puff of her tail fuzzed into scruffiness by the tangles of time. 'Kind sir, kind sir. Can you help *me*?' she drawled. 'I have been cruelly cast out and have nowhere to go.'

'B-but how? What can I . . .' Babe stammered.

'Please, please. I know you're different from the others. Those that have had their way with me

75

make their empty promises, but they're all lies . . . lies. I'm cold and afraid and terribly, terribly tired,' she droned on.

'Um . . . where is your human?' Babe asked.

'They belong to someone else now,' she said. 'Someone younger and prettier. Maybe it was my fault. Maybe if I'd tried harder . . .'

The pleas of the homeless filled Babe's ears.

'I, I, I, never even h-had a hu-hu-human,' stammered the dog with a persistent itch.

'I'm hungry,' squeaked a starving kitten with a voice more quiet than a mouse.

And so it went on. Creatures had been abandoned, dumped or otherwise left to die. And they all thought that, somehow, Babe could solve their problem.

'Kind sir . . . You were sent here for a reason,' the pink poodle asserted. 'Take pity on us. We are The Excluded and have nowhere to go.'

'Well . . . it's nice and warm inside,' Babe offered.

Bob stepped forward. 'Not a good idea,' the chimp said.

'But they . . .' Babe argued.

'No! No! Negatory! No-ness!' Bob shouted.

An old dog noticed the jar of jellybeans Bob was carrying. 'Could that be . . . food?' he barked.

The chimp clutched the jar to his chest.

'Oh Yum! Oh yumyumyumyum!' The dog

Hoggett Hollow, where our story begins.

Farmer Hoggett, moments before the big accident.

Babe and the farmer's wife set off for the city.
The mice come along for the ride.

Babe meets his first city dweller.

The Flealands Hotel.

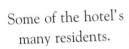
Some of the hotel's
many residents.

Babe takes in the view . . .

. . . while Tug steals Mrs Hoggett's suitcase!

Babe meets the chimps: Bob, Zootie and Easy.

The Dobermann and the Bull Terrier chase after Babe.

Babe and his newest friend.

Raiders storm the hotel.

Babe uses his nose to find his missing friends.

Babe and Ferdinand find themselves
in the middle of a fancy banquet!

Mrs Hoggett to the rescue!

The mice are happy to be home.

danced around excitedly, barking and scratching, scratching and barking.

'Have mercy. I'm faint with hunger,' the pink poodle whined.

Bob backed away.

'Food. Food. Can't remember when I last ate. Any little titbit. Just a lick. A sniff! Food! Food! Food!' the voices cried in a chorus of need.

'Quiet! Quiet!' Thelonius thundered from the balcony. The animals looked up. The old Orang-utan scanned the street, shaking his head with worry. 'You'll bring all manner of trouble.'

'Perhaps if we all went inside and lined up, I'm sure there'll be enough to go around,' Babe suggested.

Bob said gruffly, 'Hey, you're talking as if you're the Word around here.'

A low, dangerous voice growled, 'I'd say he is.'

'Who says?' Bob demanded.

A rumbling growl, and the crowd of homeless animals parted, to leave the Bull Terrier standing alone. 'I'd like to offer up a solution that I feel confident you'll all respond to . . .'

Bob was sceptical. 'Oh?'

'Whatever the Pig says . . . goes,' the Bull Terrier declared.

A silence followed. No one dared to challenge those powerful jaws.

'Anyone hostile to the notion?' the Bull Terrier demanded.

Agreement poured from every available mouth. 'Absolutely not! Whatever he says. You got it!'

'Anybody else?' the Bull Terrier asked.

Bob had not liked the look of the Bull Terrier's teeth from a distance, but up close . . . 'Fine by *moi*,' he said.

'Anybody else-else?' the Bull Terrier asked again.

All eyes turned to Thelonius. The aged ape shrugged. 'It's still just a pig.'

Like the animals seeking shelter on Noah's Ark, the homeless filed inside the Flealands Hotel. The pink poodle surveyed her surroundings. To the down-and-out dog, the shabby hotel looked like luxury.

'Oh my!' she exclaimed. 'This recalls the glory days of my youth, when I was dizzy with privilege. I had my hair styled and my nails manicured . . .'

The resident population of the Flealands Hotel regarded the visitors with suspicion. From the landing of the dog floor, Nigel sniffed. 'Riff-raff with no manners. They'll soil willy-nilly, won't they, Alan?'

The Mastiff's heavy, black head nodded. 'Willy-nilly, Nigel.'

Babe watched the last of the homeless animals

78

enter the hotel. Then he heard a gruff voice say, 'Hey, Swine . . . I want you to have this.'

Babe turned and faced the Bull Terrier. Tug had unbuckled the dog's spiked leather collar. Its sharp points shone like metal teeth in the little monkey's outstretched paw.

'Um . . . that's not necessary,' the Pig said.

'Yes it is,' the Bull Terrier insisted.

Babe did not want the mean-looking thing. 'You're very kind but . . .'

'Oh, I'm anything but kind. In fact I have a professional obligation to be malicious,' the Bull Terrier confessed.

'Then you should change jobs,' Babe suggested.

'I can't,' the dog declared.

The Pig disagreed. 'Yes, you can.'

The Bull Terrier shrugged. 'It's in the blood-line, you see. We were once warriors. Now there's just the urge . . .'

Babe shook his head. 'That's no excuse.'

The Bull Terrier looked sad. 'A murderous shadow lies hard across my soul.'

Babe was not sure he understood. 'So . . . should I have let you drown?'

'Most would have.' The Bull Terrier was still deeply confused by Babe's actions. 'Pig, if you were to wear my collar . . . it would honour me.'

*

Inside the Flealands Hotel a curious ritual was being repeated many times.

'Thank the Pig,' recited the Bull Terrier as each animal reached the front of a long, orderly queue that looped back through the hotel.

'Thank you, Pig,' each animal said while accepting a ration of jellybeans from Tug.

'You're welcome,' Babe replied.

Babe felt embarrassed when the chimps took their turn. 'Thank you, Little Thingy,' Zootie said.

But Bob just took his beans.

'Come again?' the Bull Terrier said.

Babe whispered to the dog, 'It's OK. Really.'

But the Bull Terrier was not about to let the matter rest. 'Hey, YOU!' he barked at Bob.

The chimp whispered resentfully, 'Thanks.'

'Don't mention it,' Babe replied eagerly. 'You're awfully welcome.'

Easy accepted his beans and nodded shyly at Babe. 'Thank you . . . y-y'Honour.'

In Uncle Fugly's deserted rooms, Thelonius listened glumly and dropped the last flake of food into the fish-bowl. The feisty little swimmer was still hungry – and so were all the other animals in the Flealands Hotel!

Indeed, Dear Ones, there was more than a little sniping and griping accompanying the belly-rumbles. 'I'm still hungry,' the little kitten complained.

The itchy dog scratched and moaned. 'Coupla jellybeans don't even hit the bottom.'

'If only there weren't so many of those cats!' Nigel sniffed.

To which some cats naturally took offence. Babe's attempts to stop the fight failed until the Bull Terrier shouted, 'Hey! The Pig has something to say.'

'Um ... er ... cats and dogs should be nicer to each other,' Babe said.

'Right, the Chief has spoken,' the Bull Terrier concluded. 'It is decreed that all cats and dogs shall henceforth put aside their instinctive and fanatical abhorrence of each other.'

Babe hadn't realized he'd said all that! 'Thank you,' he said.

But the Bull Terrier was not going to be stopped now. 'And that hereafter all creatures great and diminutive shall be of equal stature with rights to liberty and justice that nobody can deny and so say all of us.'

In the stunned silence that followed, the little kitten mewed, 'I'm still hungry.'

Then Zootie said, 'My tummy feels all ... thingy.'

'I know, honey,' Bob agreed. 'We did all the work. We shoulda got the most.'

Zootie moaned! She put her hand on her swollen belly. 'It hurts here,' the pregnant chimp said.

Bob put his ear to his wife's belly and listened.

'What? What's wrong?!' Easy wanted to know.

Bob smiled. 'Nothing.'

And so, Dear Ones, this topsy-turvy night was to end with a beginning . . .

Chapter 7

Sanctuary's end

This event that weaves a thread from past to future soothed the tired hearts of those assembled and, for a while at least, they put aside their uncertainties.

Something wonderful wriggled in Zootie's arms. Easy saw two tiny, fuzzy heads and four teeny flappy ears. One of the two minuscule noses let out a little sneeze.

'I'm an uncle.' Easy's eyes were wide with awe.

'Twice.' Bob could not stop staring at the double bundle.

Bob and Easy high-fived. Animals who did not have five fingers expressed their congratulations in other ways.

'Well, bite my tail!' one dog enthused.

'They've got their father's ears!' another cooed.

Thelonius watched but said nothing. The Bull

Terrier, on the other paw, addressed the assembly grandly, 'On behalf of us all, I'm sure the Chief would like to extend a special welcome. So . . . *listen up!*'

Babe did not know what to say that could possibly express the awesome joy of the occasion. So he sang. 'La, la, la. La, la, la . . .'

The Bull Terrier joined in, followed by the hungry little kitten, then by the itchy dog, until soon the entire Flealands Feline Chorus and all the other animals, homeless and residents, were singing with full-throated, merry abandon.

LA, LAAAAAA!

'Shhh!' Thelonius cautioned. But even the feisty fish had joined in the song.

LA, LA, LA, LAAAAA!

The sound travelled across the canal, between the stone canyons of skyscrapers, to the arms of an angel on top of a church. Ferdinand lifted his head and his feathers prickled with excitement. The duck knew that song. His lucky pig sang that song! Babe was near! The fowl flew off to follow that tune!

Unfortunately, Ferdinand was not the only one to hear the spontaneous miaowing, woofing and howling ode to joy. The suspicious neighbour on the other side of the canal shrilled, 'My God, Roger!

The place is teeming! Overrun with filthy animals!'

Babe threw back his head to sing even louder, and then he spotted a familiar face at the tower window. Ferdinand was tapping his beak against the glass. Babe scrambled up the stairs, followed by the Bull Terrier.

As soon as the Pig threw open the window, Ferdinand flew at him. 'Give us a peck. C'mon, Pig. Kisskisskisskiss!' The duck looked around the room. 'Who are these losers?' Then he saw the Bull Terrier. 'Who's this?'

'I'm his Conflict Resolution Consultant,' the Bull Terrier explained.

Ferdinand blinked at the spiked collar around Babe's neck. 'What's goin' on here? You look ... different.'

'Yeah, well, this place can really take it outta ya.' Babe sighed. So much had happened since he had left the Farm!

'Tell me about it,' Ferdinand agreed. 'But, hey, I'm with my pig, my lucky, lucky pig. L'il ol' Ferdie. Snug and safe at last!'

Just then, crash! A gloved hand smashed through the glass panel in the front door. In seconds the hotel was being stormed by a gang of raiders. These bullies disguised themselves in uniforms and carried badges, and they justified themselves by waving papers filled with small-

85

print. But their actions showed their true colours.

One was a doctor. She wore a starched white lab coat over her flowered dress. 'Check upstairs,' she told a muscular motorcycle policeman.

One man wearing protective padding bent to stroke a cat who was leaning against him lovingly.

The man's partner offered food pellets to the pink poodle. 'Ooh, well bite my tail,' she cooed. She pranced on her hind legs for the tall, gangly man, then rolled over on her back.

'Doll. Don't go there,' the Bull Terrier muttered under his breath. The bully knew a bully when he saw one. But the pink poodle was a fool for food. Tail wagging, she allowed herself to be led out of the door.

'No one home!' the motorcycle cop called from upstairs.

One of the raiders put up a NOTICE OF IMPOUNDMENT on the front door.

Ferdinand panicked! 'Feet! Feet! Time to retreat!' The frantic fowl ran straight into the motorcycle cop, who grabbed him by the neck.

The cruel cop chuckled. 'Hey . . . supper!'

Babe was not a violent pig. But in defence of his friend, he did his best Bull Terrier imitation: 'Rarrrgh!' Babe charged towards the leather-clad cop.

86

The cop laughed, easily snatching up the defenceless Pig. 'Yo . . . breakfast!'

But the laugh was short-lived . . . because this time a real Bull Terrier came bounding at him! The cop reached for his gun, but the dog was already snapping at his throat!

Another of the raiders ran to the rescue. The huge, padded man leapt over the Pig and started pounding the Bull Terrier with his truncheon.

Cats and dogs poured out of the hotel from every possible exit, scattering over the rooftops and into the streets. Some reached freedom. Others were scooped up as they made their break.

The motorcycle policeman rubbed his neck as he came down the stairs. He was glad to see his colleague dragging away his attacker. The Bull Terrier's savage jaws were restrained by a metal muzzle bristling with buckles and a shiny, steel lock.

Babe watched helplessly. Behind him a lampshade trembled. Feathers decorated the lamp's peculiar base, which consisted of a pair of shivering duck legs.

The animals could do nothing against this gang of humans armed with tranquillizer gun, darts and nets. Though Bob tried desperately to defend his babies, several darts hit him and he fell, senseless.

Zootie looked up at Thelonius and begged, 'Please, Thelonius! Do something!'

The Orang-utan turned away. On his way back to Fugly's rooms, Thelonius passed Babe. He stared into those twinkly little pig eyes and spat out, 'You did this!'

Easy, Zootie and the twins were cruelly captured. Then another of the raiders threw open the door of Fugly's room. 'Get a load of this!' he called to his companions.

The other invaders peered through the door, to see Thelonius standing in the centre of the room. The Orang-utan held Fugly's blanket, a small suitcase and the fish-bowl. He looked like the perfect English butler, packed and ready for a trip.

Babe watched the raiders advance on Thelonius. 'Careful,' one of them cautioned. 'They're incredibly strong.'

Another raider slunk around behind the beast. At a nod, they all rushed at the Orang-utan. One of them threw a net over Thelonius. In the process, the man bumped into the fish-bowl, which smashed on the floor.

As the men dragged Thelonius away, the feisty little fish was flapping in a puddle, sparkling between shards of broken glass.

'Mercy . . . mercy . . .' he gasped.

Babe hurried to the desperate fish. As he tried

to work out what to do, a noose dropped around Babe's neck!

The raider was already loaded down with several cats, but the big, padded man dragged Babe behind him by the lead. The Pig glanced back to see the poor fish still flapping on the floor.

The miserable prisoners formed a sad parade down the steps of the Flealands Hotel. In the Landlady's room a few animals still enjoyed their freedom, but not for long!

'Aa-ah-choo!' Ferdinand sneezed. 'Are there any cats in here?' he asked in a nasal voice.

'Cats? No way!' Flealick snapped. 'No cat would dare come in here!'

'But I'm allergic to ca-cA-A-AH-CHOO!' Ferdinand's words turned into a violent sneeze. 'I'm telling ya, there are *cats* in here.'

In his haste to rid the room of the hated species, Flealick forgot who the real enemy was.

As he passed the Landlady's door, the motorcycle cop heard the muffled barks and yowls of a cat-and-dog fight. The officer marched inside and lifted the bed. A duck, a dog-on-wheels and a dozen cats froze in shock on a battlefield littered with fur and feathers.

With a skitter of claws, the creatures scattered. Ferdinand shot out between the cop's black leather boots. Flealick scooted for the door, but then he felt his wheels leave the ground. He struggled, but the lame dog was no match for the motorcycle cop!

Nigel and Alan crept out of their hiding place in the wardrobe. The big dogs looked around in panic.

'Flealick! Flealick!' the Bulldog called.

His huge Mastiff companion shook like a chihua-hua in a blizzard. 'Flealick's gone, Nigel!' Alan barked. Everything that meant safety, home, comfort and companionship had suddenly gone!

Ferdinand was intent on making his escape. Unfortunately, as he cleared the corner of the second-floor landing, the duck ran straight into a raider's legs. Webbed, orange feet squeaked on the floor as he performed an abrupt change of direction. Ferdinand launched himself through the rails of the banister, down towards the ground floor.

Luckily, the duck landed slap on another raider's head! The big guy dragging Babe was so startled that he bumped into a bookcase, *thud*! The book-case crashed into a table, *thump*! and knocked over a vase, *crash*! and a potted plant, *crack*!

In the confusion, Babe broke free. The handle of the lead thumped up the stairs behind him as the Pig raced up to Fugly's room.

Babe skidded across the floor to the puddle and quickly slurped up the still-flapping fish. The three mice did not understand what the Pig was up to. OK, he was hungry, but this was hardly the time . . .

Babe ran to the open kitchen window, took careful aim, and *thwoo*! spat the fish out and into the canal . . . plop!

The fish breathed in the cool water all around him. He flapped his fins and wriggled his tail. He did not mind the bits of chewing-gum wrapper or the occasional bottle top. The fish was free at last! Yes, Dear Ones, he was alive, swimming, and free at last!

Tug gave Babe the thumbs-up sign. But the Pig had no time to feel proud for saving the fish. The big raider came thundering into the room!

Babe's eyes darted around for some means of escape. The answer came to him: follow the fish! The Pig clambered up to the window. He dived towards the canal, but the raider lunged after him. The big man's hands managed to grab the collar. Babe dangled over the side.

Then the raider jumped! Something had pinched his bottom! The big man tumbled out of the window and into the canal!

Tug laughed. Dear Ones, perhaps you've already guessed whose little hands had pinched that big bottom.

In the alley behind the hotel, a van was parked

behind an official car and a police motorcycle. Nigel and Alan watched the raiders load their live loot into cages inside the van. Nigel spotted Flealick's chequered flag as a raider handed the little dog to a human inside the van.

The big dogs did not know what to do! Could they possibly hope to overcome so many humans? Perhaps there would be a chance for escape later. Whatever happened, they could not abandon Flealick! Who would make sure he didn't roll too fast? Who would remind him to take his medicine and lick behind his ears? The loyal friends exchanged a look, then leapt into the back of the van.

At that moment, a voice inside the van grumbled, 'This one's useless. Look at him.'

Rough hands tossed the lame dog out of the van. Meanwhile other hands were slamming the doors shut. Nigel and Alan were trapped inside!

Flealick went wild! The little dog snapped at the nearest ankles, which happened to belong to the doctor. She snatched up her lab coat and launched a kick at Flealick.

The raider who'd gone after Babe came, dripping, out of the shadows. The padding which had protected him from the Bull Terrier squished with each step as he angrily made his way to the official car.

'Don't even ask!' he told his partner.

His gangly companion shrugged. It had been a strange shift. Even in the big City you didn't see Orang-utans wearing butler's suits every night.

From the safety of the shadows, a wet pig and a small monkey watched the vehicles depart. The doctor had not been entirely successful in kicking away Flealick. In fact, because the persistent pooch was still tugging at the hem of her dress, the doctor deliberately slammed it in the van's door as she climbed aboard.

Flealick clung to that strip of flowered cloth – and would not let go!

Babe stepped out of the shadows. What was Flealick doing? The little dog would get himself killed!

'Flealick, let go!' Babe shouted. '*Let go!*'

Babe turned to Tug. The two started chasing the van.

On the roof of the Flealands Hotel, Ferdinand moaned, 'Pig. Pig. Whaddaya doing to me?'

The duck did not care what happened to the little dog or to any of the other strange creatures he had met at the hotel. But Ferdinand could not lose his lucky Pig.

Flealick was lucky he did not get run over. The van swerved. The dog's wheels burned rubber! The dress ripped just a little more with each bend in the road. Every second, Flealick was flung closer to the van's massive back wheels!

Babe and Tug could not keep up with the speeding vehicles. They trotted breathlessly after the convoy, fearing greatly for the fate of their senseless friend. Yes, Dear Ones, you may recall that Flealick's sense of smell was poor and his eyesight failing; and, as for hitching a ride on a speeding hem, well, that certainly rates as risky, if not downright stupid.

Perhaps because the dog's intentions were noble, or because the doctor did not buy the best dresses, before the tyres could crush the canine's cranium, when the van turned a corner the hem was ripped off!

Flealick was hurtled across the deserted main road. Tumble crash bang! The little dog bounced head over wheels into an empty back street.

Babe's collar clattered as he turned the corner and saw a most horrible sight.

Flealick lay flat on his back in the gutter. One wonky wheel spun slowly, but otherwise the frail figure lay perfectly still.

Babe feared the worst. 'Flealick? Flealick?' The Pig licked the dog's nose. One red eye opened. Babe tried again, 'Can you hear me?'

Flealick's dazed reply was muffled by a mouthful of flowered cloth.

'Huh?' Babe asked.

Tug removed the cloth.

94

'Don't worry,' Flealick said faintly. 'I got their scent. Flip me over.'

'Are you OK?' Babe asked anxiously.

'Yeah. Yeah. Hurry, hurry!' Flealick barked impatiently.

Tug and Babe pulled Flealick upright. The little dog shook his head, trying to clear it. 'Feelin' good. Feelin' peppy!' he said.

Flealick snuffled the air.

'They went this-a-way,' he declared, pointing his clogged nose back towards the hotel.

Babe inhaled deeply. 'Actually, Flealick . . . I think it's that way.'

Ferdinand flapped his wings hysterically. 'Wait a minute. Whaddaya doing?'

Babe felt proud. 'It's all in the hooter, Ferdie, the schnoz.' The beagle at the airport had been right. Babe *did* have a good nose. And the time had come for him to use it!

'The what?' Ferdinand demanded.

'The olfactory instrument,' Babe explained calmly.

The duck became even more hysterical. 'Pig. Pig, you're unravelling here. Pull yourself together and listen to reason. A. They're long gone. B. They were not nice people. C is for Kamikaze. And D is for Delusional – which is what you are in the head!'

Dear Ones, you probably noticed that C is not

the first letter in the word *Kamikaze*. You may also recall what the old sheepdog, Rex, told Babe about listening to the Duck. Babe remembered the wise dog saying, 'Don't take counsel of your fears.'

'Ferdie,' Babe began.

Ferdinand fumed, 'Face it. You're just a little Pig in the big city! What can you possibly do?! What can *anyone* do? *Why even try?*'

Babe wondered if the duck was right. Maybe one little Pig could not make a difference. Maybe Babe couldn't even save his own skin, much less anyone else's.

Then the Pig heard something squeak. He turned and saw a lame, half-blind dog with no sense of smell rolling his dented harness along the street to save his friends.

Babe considered his options. Then he turned to Tug. 'Would you help me off with this, please?'

Tug lifted the collar over Babe's pinkish head. The Pig trotted after Flealick.

The duck sighed as he followed his friend. 'Ferdinand the Duck. Witness to insanity.'

Chapter 8

Where do we belong?

Sometimes we discover our talents only through necessity. Babe, who had never used his nose for anything but the pursuit of food, soon found he could make his way through the trickiest of smellscapes.

The rich, chocolatey aroma of freshly ground coffee drifted towards his nostrils, blending with sweet bakery smells and the salty odour of a fish market. Each alley, each passing truck and perfumed pedestrian, brought new scents for Babe's sensitive snout. The sights and sounds of the city, its gleaming towers and rushing rivers of traffic, faded as the Pig focused on that single sense.

Eventually, Babe came to feel so in tune with his hooter that he half-believed it was talking to him.

His snout wasn't as loud as his belly had been, but its small voice was quite clear. Finally, the Pig's pink proboscis announced, 'I do believe we're here.'

And sure enough when the animals turned the next corner . . .

'Ta-daaa!' Babe's snout crowed triumphantly.

The raiders' van was parked outside a building in the University Hospital complex. Babe's nose led the four friends to a window in one of the large, modern buildings where lights were flashing.

While Ferdinand, Flealick and Babe hid in some bushes, Tug climbed up a drainpipe and peeped inside. A photographer was snapping mug shots of the Flealands residents. Thelonius was standing against a measuring board. His clothes had been removed. The chimps, also undressed, and the other animals watched from their cages.

Flash! The human photographed Thelonius's left profile. He pushed the ape's chin the other way.

Flash! The photographer snapped Thelonius's right profile.

Then he turned his flashing camera on the new-born chimps.

Tug looked into another window and saw another horror: rows and rows of rabbits, their heads poking out of metal boxes.

Tug scrambled back down to join Babe, Flealick

and Ferdinand. The little monkey was gesturing wildly and gibbering hysterically.

'Let's go get 'em!' Flealick started rolling out of the bushes, but Babe stuck a trotter between the spokes of the dog's wheels.

At that moment, two humans in lab coats strolled past the animals. The four friends held their breath.

When the people had passed, Babe cautioned the others, 'If we get caught, we won't be able to help anybody.'

Esme Cordelia Hoggett was caught in an extremely difficult position. Dear Ones, you can't already have forgotten the disaster that befell the poor Farmer's Wife when she went looking for Babe?

Covered in glue from head to toe, Mrs Hoggett had been arrested, interrogated and examined, then forced to sleep in a windowless cell with a snoring criminal. Yet none of this pained her as much as knowing that she had failed in her mission.

But at last the Farmer's Wife had her day in court. In a wood-panelled room dedicated to justice, Mrs Hoggett explained her view of things. 'I've given myself a good hard talking to. I said, "Esme, you've let Arthur down. You've let yourself down. And you've let the Pig down. What are you, Esme Hoggett, if you can't look after a helpless

99

creature that has been placed in your care and trusts you?"'

She looked at the judge. 'Sir, I put to you a simple question. What is the worth of a pig? As a general rule, I used to dismiss pigs. But a pig became my husband's best friend. And I have to confess that made me a little jealous. But not any more. So, go ahead, lock me in jail! Bind me in chains! The minute I am free, I shall march straight back into the streets and continue my search!'

The judge had never heard anyone speak so many words in so short a time. Evidently, this was a woman of clear conscience and good intent. Besides, the judge had grown up on a farm with many pink pals. The twinkling eyes in his round, pink face showed that the judge had a fondness for pigs . . . but that's another story.

The judge pounded his gavel. 'Case dismissed!'

Thanks to the cautious Pig, the animals were able to find a way in to the research building. They waited until most of the staff had left, then they crept to the room where their friends were being kept.

Tug's tiny paw turned the door handle.

Babe looked into the dark room. 'Hello?' the Pig called.

'It's the Pinkness!' Bob exclaimed.

'It's the thingy!' Zootie added.

The Bull Terrier barked, 'Chief!'

The pink poodle sighed. 'I knew he'd come.'

'Shh!' Babe whispered. 'We have to be quiet.'

But the animals were excited. Tug quickly set the chimps free. Together, they released the cats and dogs from their cages.

The Bull Terrier managed to speak around his muzzle. 'Chief, I'm proud of ya.'

The other animals were soon surrounding Babe, eager to express their gratitude to the Pig.

From his hiding place beneath the stairwell, Flealick watched two technicians load a cage on to a truck.

'I'll just lock up,' one of them said.

Flealick panicked as he watched the technician make his way back into the building.

Meanwhile Ferdinand was trying to save his feathers. 'OK, OK,' he said. 'You all know the term "Survival of the Fastest"? Well, I got an idea. We split into two groups. The fast ones come with me. The slow ones stay behind and sacrifice themselves.'

'Ferdinand!' Babe protested.

'Well, that way we don't all die,' the duck explained. 'I think that's only reasonable, don't you?'

Babe turned to the group. 'May I suggest we stay

calm, maintain a tight formation, and proceed in an orderly fashion.'

Ferdinand panicked. 'And may he suggest we do it real fast!'

'Where's Thelonius?' Easy asked.

The Orang-utan was in the corner, pulling on his shirt.

'Whaddaya doing?' Bob asked him.

'I . . . I'm not dressed,' Thelonius stated.

Babe said gently, 'Mr Thelonius. Time to go.'

'But . . . I'm not . . . dressed,' he protested.

Zootie said, 'Thelonius, you're an Oranguthingy.'

The ape did not know what to do. In truth, Dear Ones, Thelonius did not even know what he was. Was he an Oranguthingy or a human? A butler, a performer, or an ape? He stood frozen in indecision.

A clock ticked on the wall.

In the stairwell, Flealick cursed his wheels. He watched helplessly as the returning technician neared the top of the stairs.

Suddenly the animals in the room could hear footsteps.

'Quiet! Quiet!' Nigel woofed softly.

'Shoosh!' Alan added.

They scattered into the darkest corners of the

102

room. Easy pulled Thelonius with him. They all held their breath in fear.

The technician opened the door, glanced inside, rubbed his eyes and yawned. Then he pulled the door shut and locked it behind him. When they heard the steps recede, the animals breathed again. Thelonius slowly put on his coat.

One door closed, and across town another opened. Mrs Hoggett entered the Flealands Hotel and was shocked by the wreckage. She picked her way over the broken glass from the front door and glanced up at the NOTICE OF IMPOUNDMENT.

On her way upstairs, she saw the broken vase and the potted plant that had been tipped over when Ferdinand had startled one of the raiders. Water from the vase had mixed with soil from the plant.

Mrs Hoggett stopped in her tracks. There were footprints in the mud. She bent down to get a closer look and her glue-starched dress split with a loud *raiiiippp*!

Mrs Hoggett didn't care. The tracks had definitely been made by the trotters of a pig.

'Pig?' Mrs Hoggett called. 'Pig? Pig, pig, pig!'

The Farmer's Wife followed the trail into Uncle Fugly's living-room. The Landlady was there, slumped in a chair by the window.

'Is the Pig here?' Mrs Hoggett asked.

'Gone,' the Landlady said. Her lips barely moved, her chest hardly lifted to take breath and her eyes looked dull and lifeless.

'But he was here?' the Farmer's Wife persisted.

'They've all gone,' the Landlady reported in a hollow voice. 'Every last one of them.'

Mrs Hoggett shook her head. 'What happened, dear?'

The Landlady's head sagged even lower. 'This used to be such a lovely neighbourhood. People caring, keeping an eye out for each other. They really did. What's the world coming to? I'm away one night, just one night, with my Uncle Fugly on his deathbed!'

The Landlady burst into tears.

The Farmer's Wife hugged the stranger. The Landlady's ear pressed against Mrs Hoggett's glue-hardened dress.

The Landlady poured out all her pain. 'It's all my fault. I thought I could make a true place, a kind place where they could be OK. But how can you do that here? It was stupid for me to even try. And now . . . Fugly's gone, but . . . but I wasn't *so* stupid, was I? Because we have to belong some-where, don't we?'

Mrs Hoggett patted the Landlady's back. 'Dear, who did this?' she asked gently.

104

'What did the animals ever do to her?' the Land-lady wondered.

'Who?' the Farmer's Wife wanted to know.

'Her! That . . .' Anger gave the Landlady new life. She pointed across the canal and shouted, '*Her!*'

Mrs Hoggett leapt to her feet – and her dress broke apart! The slabs of glued fabric *thunked* to the floor.

'Right!' Mrs Hoggett said. 'Clothes! Got anything that will fit me?'

A few moments later, Mrs Hoggett came charging out of the Flealands Hotel dressed in Fugly Floom's clown's suit! She was dragging the Land-lady behind her.

Imagine the opera-loving, animal-hating neigh-bour's surprise on being roused from a sound sleep by the Farmer's Wife dressed as a clown! When they answered the door, Mrs Hoggett screamed: 'WE WANT OUR ANIMALS!'

At that moment, those self-same animals were making their way up a teetering pyramid of cages, boxes, stools and chairs leading to a trapdoor in the ceiling of the research building. Unlike the tower Babe had climbed in Uncle Fugly's kitchen, this was no cruel prank. Shaky though it was, the pyramid was the only means of escape for the

Flealands animals and their homeless companions.

Once the pyramid had been negotiated, the animals had to cross an air-conditioning pipe connecting the research laboratory to another hospital building. The Pig led the way.

Towards the front of the line, the itchy dog scratched himself nervously. 'So where are we going?' he asked.

The pink poodle didn't know. 'Does it matter? In this whole wide world is there anywhere that's truly, really safe?'

'Yeah, for my babies?' Zootie asked; the little twins had already been through so much in their short lives.

'Well, there is a place I know where everyone is inclined to be fair and good to each other,' Babe said thoughtfully. 'But it's ever so far away, and I'm not even sure it's there any more.'

In this place of steel pipes and steelier hearts, the little Pig struggled to recall the green hills and warm hearts of home. He thought of a bandaged hand reaching out to scratch his head, and a certain soft voice that had once uttered the words, 'That'll do, Pig. That'll do.'

'I think he's talking about the "Fun",' Easy explained to Zootie.

All the animals had crossed the pipe except Nigel

and Flealick. Flealick, because of his wheels, had remained on the ground floor. But Nigel . . .

The Bulldog looked down at the ground, far below him. 'Alan! Alan!' he called. The Bulldog's sturdy legs were frozen in fear.

Babe recognized a situation that called for firmness, as occasionally happened with the sheep back home. 'Nigel. Get your big bottom over here,' the Pig said.

Nigel tried to get a grip. 'I'm making a fool of myself, aren't I, Alan? I'm absolutely rigid with anxiety, aren't I? I can't do it, can I, Alan?'

For the first time in their long friendship, the Mastiff disagreed. 'Yes you can, Nigel!'

Through his muzzle, the Bull Terrier said, 'Nige, you're a big brave wolf, bred for battle against the brute, the beast, the bear and the bull!'

The Bulldog shook his massive, tan-coloured head. 'I'm not a wolf. I'm just a big fat scaredy-cat!'

The hungry little kitten spoke up. 'That's it,' he said. 'Think cat. Pretend you're a cat.' The tiny kitten, like all the other felines, had crossed the narrow bridge with complete confidence.

Babe saw the wisdom in the little cat's strategy. 'Yes, Nigel. You're a cat!'

The ugly, muscle-bound dog repeated dutifully, 'I'm a cat. I'm a very graceful . . .' He stretched one paw daintily on to the pipe. '... svelte...' Nigel took another step into the void. '... sure-footed pussycat.'

The Bulldog took two more steps, then panicked. 'What if I fall?!'

For a moment, no one said a word. Then Ferdinand piped up, 'Pretend you're a birdy.'

Babe shot the duck a look.

'You're a cat! A custard-pipe, Pig-dog, Dog-cat,' the stuttering dog exclaimed.

'I'm a cat,' Nigel repeated. 'I'm a cat. I'm a cat. I'm a cat...' Slowly the Bulldog inched his way across the rest of the pipe.

The entire assembly sighed with relief as Nigel and Alan were reunited.

'Yeah,' said the Bull Terrier. 'Now wasn't that great for your self-esteem?'

Nigel turned to the Mastiff. 'It was, wasn't it, Alan?'

The big black dog was glad to be in agreement once more. 'Darn tootin', Nigel!'

The pink poodle gazed dreamily at the Bull Terrier. 'Would you like to work on my self-esteem?' she asked the big dog.

Only one little boy was awake when the escapees entered the darkened Children's Ward. The animals had made their way from the research wing across the pipe to the hospital building where sick children were tended.

The child was the sole witness to a moonlit parade led by a pig. Chimpanzees, dogs, cats and a duck made their way quietly past the sleeping patients towards the lift that would take them down to freedom.

The little boy's jaw dropped in wonder when the last animal stopped and stared straight at him! Though he loved animals and was always reading about them in books, the child had never seen an orang-utan. The sad truth is, Dear Ones, that the boy had not seen much beyond the inside of doctors' offices. But on that magical night, by the glow of the moon, the delighted child saw an orang-utan in a butler's uniform. Pain, fear and illness were forgotten. The boy smiled!

If he had looked out of the window at that moment, the child would have seen something even more amazing. The resourceful Farmer's Wife and the animal-loving Landlady had used the only means of transportation at hand: Uncle Fugly's trick tandem bicycle!

Exhausted from pedalling through traffic, the women had finally hitched a ride by clinging to the back of an ambulance. With each turn of the trick bicycle's wheels, the riders bounced up and down like demented engine-pistons.

The brightly-coloured van screamed into the hospital complex, the tandem in tow. The women bounced past various buildings, including one buzzing with activity. Sleek limousines gleamed beneath strands of fairy lights, their doors opening to let out women in glittering gowns and men in shiny top hats.

Suddenly Mrs Hoggett saw the sign she was looking for: RESEARCH LABORATORY. She let go of the ambulance, and the bike veered off.

As the bouncing ladies passed underneath the air-conditioning pipe, a little dog rolled out of the shadows, barking frantically.

While Mrs Hoggett and the Landlady were following Flealick, the little boy trailed after the animal parade. He padded to the lift at the end of the hall and pounded on the door.

The night nurse walked up to him. 'Gosh, little man. What are you doing here?' she asked him.

The little boy pointed at the lift and said, 'Duck.'

The nurse had never heard such nonsense in her life. She scooped up the child in her arms and took him back to bed.

Of course, the boy was right. There *was* a duck in the lift, as well as an Orang-utan, several chimps, cats, dogs, one tiny monkey and a pig, all on their way to the ground floor – and freedom!

On the next floor the lift doors whirred open

again. A doctor chatting with a couple in evening dress did not notice the lift doors open behind him. The group of escapees held their breaths!

But the man continued chatting, intent on his fund-raising. The doors glided shut. The escapees breathed again and descended to the next floor.

Flealick had never been particularly good at finding things, and now he led Mrs Hoggett and the Landlady to a dead-end!

In the quiet corridor, the women saw a kitchen helper drinking coffee.

'Evening,' he said.

'We're looking for some . . . er . . . animals,' Mrs Hoggett said.

'What kind?'

'Pig. Cats. Dogs. Monkeys . . . that sort of thing.'

The man just stared. 'Uh-huh.'

At that moment, the lift reached its destination. The doors opened and the animals found themselves looking into a busy kitchen where the Chef was balancing an armload of pots and pans. The Chef was a large, red-faced man with a hot temper. He saw the animals, screamed and then dropped the pots with a loud crash!

Mrs Hoggett and the Landlady heard the sound of clattering pots, shouting men, barking dogs and . . . a *pig squealing*!

Flealick shot between the man's legs. Mrs Hoggett and the Landlady nearly knocked him down in their haste to enter the kitchen.

Chefs and waiters were chasing the creatures around the crowded kitchen. The animals were fleeing through another door.

Mrs Hoggett's chubby legs pumped faster than anyone would have thought possible. She had almost caught up with the animals when the Chef grabbed her by the trick braces that held her clown's baggy pants up.

'Pig! Pig!' Mrs Hoggett shouted.

As he ran through the door, Babe glanced over his shoulder and saw a vision: the Boss's Wife was running towards him wearing a bright costume. Her braces stretched and stretched until her fingers could almost touch Babe's bristly white fur.

Then, suddenly, she shot backwards! The trick braces had reached their limit and snap! Mrs Hoggett found herself back in the kitchen! The door slammed shut. The vision was gone.

But Babe's faith was restored. The Boss's Wife was here! The Farm was real. There was hope!

'It's *her*!' Babe squealed joyfully.

Thelonius was similarly moved by the round figure in the bright clown's costume. 'Himself,' the awestruck ape said to Easy. 'I thought I saw ... Himself.'

'Ferdie! The Boss's Wife. She's here!' Babe exclaimed.

But the Duck wasn't listening. 'Er, Pig? Can I borrow you for a moment?' he said.

Babe turned and saw for the first time where they were. They had run from the kitchen straight into a gigantic ballroom! Seated on gilded velvet chairs around laden tables were the city's wealthiest citizens, some wearing jewels and satins, others elegant black dinner jackets.

'Well, bite my tail!' the pink poodle declared with pleasure.

'This must be the "fun",' Easy said.

To one side was a mountain of food. Chefs in crisp, white uniforms stood proudly beside their masterpieces.

Beyond them, a nervous waiter was perched on a tall ladder beside his carefully constructed pyramid of champagne glasses.

The room was deadly quiet as the banquet guests stared at the animals.

On stage, the Grand Matriarch held in her hands a huge, cardboard cheque. She was frozen in the act of presenting the cheque to a man in a dinner jacket.

Hoping the animals were just part of the entertainment, she finally managed to say, 'Oh . . . what a surprise. I adore surprises.'

113

Back on the dance floor, chefs, waiters and a few helpful guests slowly advanced on the animals, trying to shoo them back into the kitchen.

But Ferdinand had no wish to return to that room full of cleavers and sauces! The duck made a dash for the tables. The others followed his lead, scattering in all directions!

Babe ran towards a group of ladies and hid among the billowing folds of their flowing gowns, with Ferdinand right behind him.

Bob's only thought was for the safety of his children. With Zootie clutching the twins, Bob cleared a path to the balcony. The Chimp hoped the upper level would be safe from the shrieking, flailing Humans crowding the main floor.

But as Zootie climbed up a column, the balcony's fire-doors burst open! Mrs Hoggett and the Landlady were standing there, back to back, blasting at the pursuing kitchen staff with fire-extinguishers.

'Please, try to stay calm,' the Grand Matriarch called out, above the cries of the crowd around her.

Tug suddenly jumped up on her lectern.

'Arrgh!' the Grand Matriarch screamed. 'Security! Call security!'

Meanwhile, up on the balcony, Mrs Hoggett turned to the Landlady. 'Are you with me on this?' she called out over the roar of her fire-extinguisher.

'All the way, Esme!' the Landlady replied.

Mrs Hoggett continued to hold off the kitchen staff while the Landlady raced down the stairs to the dance floor. Then the Farmer's Wife made her way to the edge of the balcony.

'Come, Pig!' she called. *'Come, Pig!'*

Babe and Ferdinand emerged from between two frothy ball-gowns and looked up to find the source of the voice.

Thelonius also stared up at the brightly clad figure. 'It looks like Himself,' he said.

Easy shook his head. 'Thelonius, it isn't.'

Whoever it was, the clown was in trouble! Mrs Hoggett had waiters behind her, guests in front of her, and crazed kitchen staff in between. There was only one way out!

Mrs Hoggett climbed up on to the balcony rail, took hold of one of the golden sashes hanging from the room's big crystal chandelier, and launched herself into space!

A waiter reached out to grab her, but only managed to catch a corner of a trick handkerchief. It streamed out of her back pocket like a long, multi-coloured tail.

Babe watched as the Farmer's Wife swung across the room and landed on the balcony on the other side. 'Ferdie,' he said to the duck, 'things are looking up!'

But the duck was not so sure. 'Don't cross your bridges before they hatch,' he replied.

And the duck was right! Before Babe knew what had happened, he'd been scooped up by the furious Chef!

Just then, the Landlady emerged from the crowd. 'That your pig?' she demanded. 'I don't think so!'

She tried to take Babe from the Chef, while Ferdinand pecked at his feet. But some waiters suddenly appeared and grabbed the Landlady from behind!

The cheering of the crowd was cut short by a cry from above. Mrs Hoggett had tied the golden sash to her trick braces. She looked out over the crowd and shouted, 'I AM ESME CORDELIA HOGGETT! AND I'VE COME FOR MY ARTHUR'S PIG!'

With all eyes upon her, Mrs Hoggett launched herself off the balcony and bungee-jumped straight for Babe!

Unfortunately, Mrs Hoggett had never bungee-jumped before. She missed her target and bounced back up to the balcony with only the Chef's hat. The Chef turned and made for the kitchen doors, Babe still in his arms.

Mrs Hoggett soared once more across the wide ballroom. Bouncing from table to table like a weightless astronaut, the Farmer's Wife finally landed on a food-trolley. Mrs Hoggett gave the metal surfboard a push and it rolled across the room – straight into the Chef's back!

The Chef hurtled through the air into a crowded table. Babe was thrown free! He came to rest in a mountain of creamy cakes.

'Come, Pig!' Mrs Hoggett called as she bounced around the ballroom. 'Come, Pig!'

Smeared with pudding and a bit lost, Babe staggered away from the dessert table.

'Incoming! Incoming!' Ferdinand squawked.

Babe looked up just in time to avoid the Chef, who was charging across the dance floor. The crazed Chef jumped up on a table and grabbed hold of Mrs Hoggett's legs!

Above them, the huge chandelier creaked ominously. It had not been built to support a bouncing clown or a mad chef. And, at that moment, it was also sheltering Bob, Zootie and the twins. Small fragments of plaster drifted down on their heads as they held on tight.

Below them, the Chef clung to Mrs Hoggett's shoes. Her trick stockings stretched and stretched until her legs looked more than twice as long as the rest of her! Then the Chef started to swing her around by her stockings, faster and faster!

'We have to stop him, Ferdie!' Babe exclaimed.

The Pig charged across the dance floor, straight into the Chef's knees. The Chef fell backwards, yanking her stockings right off of Mrs Hoggett!

The Farmer's Wife went flying towards the pyramid of champagne glasses, which were still being guarded by the very nervous waiter. He ducked in time to avoid being smashed into by Mrs Hoggett, his ladder wobbling. But the waiter recovered his balance just in time for Mrs Hoggett's return swing . . .

Ooof! The Farmer's Wife crashed right into him. The waiter toppled off his ladder and fell into the mountain of food. As he scrambled to his feet, he found a piece of the clown's suit in his hand, a big yellow tag that said 'DO NOT PULL'.

The waiter looked up to see the Farmer's Wife blowing up like a giant balloon! As Mrs Hoggett bounced around the room, Babe chased after her. But before he could reach her, three security guards came racing in through the main doors! Mrs Hoggett watched as a couple of waiters herded the Pig towards the security guards. He was surrounded!

As Mrs Hoggett prepared to swing to Babe's rescue, the Chef climbed up to the opposite balcony and grabbed his own golden sash. He was ready to intercept her!

The Farmer's Wife jumped.

The Chef jumped . . . and slammed into her! Mrs Hoggett bounced, out of control, barely making the opposite balcony.

Suddenly, Thelonius swung into action. The Orang-utan climbed up to the nearest balcony, took hold of a sash, and swung across the room to land right next to Mrs Hoggett.

The Farmer's Wife looked up at the strange creature. Thelonius stared back. Finally Mrs Hoggett managed a shy smile.

Then she heard a squeal. The security guards had caught Babe! The Pig was being carried, wriggling and squealing, towards an exit. The Landlady and the rest of the animals were blocking the way, but how long could they hold out?

And now the Chef had been joined on the opposite balcony by a waiter and a guest, each holding a golden sash and ready to jump.

Mrs Hoggett let out a wild yell and started her swing. But at the last moment Thelonius reached out and grabbed her, holding her back. It was too late for the three men; they were already swinging across the room. They swooped past ahead of Mrs Hoggett and Thelonius, giving the two a clear path to Babe.

The security guard carrying the Pig looked up in time to see Esme Cordelia Hoggett descending upon him like a force of nature. The Farmer's Wife grabbed Babe and soared away as the Chef, the waiter and the guest collided with one another in mid-air and fell to the ground!

The Farmer's Wife and the Farmer's Pig were reunited at last! The two did a victory lap around the room, followed by a swinging Orang-utan and a flying Duck. The Landlady and the other animals beamed with pride. Even the crowd of guests cheered!

If only the weight of the Orang-utan, the Pig and the Farmer's Wife had not finally overloaded the chandelier. With a *crunch*, it tore away from its moorings!

Bob and Zootie gave a cry and quickly jumped on to a nearby net holding thousands of balloons. The net slipped its moorings and the chimps rode it to safety. Mrs Hoggett and Babe bounced clear as the chandelier crashed to the ground!

In the shocked moment of silence that followed, thousands of balloons floated gently down. Slowly the guests began emerging from under tables. Faces used to frowning at board meetings were alive with smiles.

On stage, Tug began playing with the balloons, batting them this way and that. Across the room, the pink poodle found the handsome Bull Terrier lying on the ground. She licked his ear.

'Oh Big Guy, are you OK?' she asked.

The Bull Terrier thought he was dreaming: that soft voice, that pink fur!

He opened his eyes. 'I am now ... my little Fumphful.'

But misery is often the neighbour of happiness. A few feet away, Zootie was searching through the debris of the broken chandelier. She was frantic.

'One of the babies is missing!' she said.

Babe looked up at the tall ceiling. High above, in the hole where the chandelier used to be, the Pig saw something move. He squinted his eyes. Babe could just make out a tiny ball of dark fur. The baby Chimp was clinging to a fragment of plaster!

Suddenly, the little fellow sneezed, and the plaster started to crumble.

'Thelonius!' Babe shouted

Across the room, directly under the little chimp, the Orang-utan was helping Mrs Hoggett to her feet.

Babe ran over to them. *'Thelonius!'*

The Orang-utan turned to the Pig just as Babe cried, 'Look!'

With one final tiny squeeze, the plaster broke! The baby plummeted towards the ground. Somewhere, a woman screamed.

'What?' Thelonius said.

'Look up!' Babe shouted.

Thelonius looked up at the ceiling and, at the last moment, thrust out his arms.

121

Plop! The tiny Chimp landed safely in Thelonius's hands.

Up on stage, the Grand Matriarch let out a little sigh. 'Much more exciting than last year,' she said. Her twinkling, beady eyes looked very much like a pig's . . .

Zootie turned up from the tiny twins who were resting in her arms. 'Thank you,' she said to Thelonius.

'Yeah, Thelonius. Thank you,' Bob added.

Thelonius stared at Bob, then said, 'Thank the Pig.'

The Flealands Hotel would never be the same. Coloured lights pulsed in time to the music pouring out through its freshly painted windows. A bold neon sign read: DANCELANDS.

The neighbours across the canal turned up the volume of their opera, but they couldn't drown out the noise.

'We were better off with the animals, Hortense,' the man said.

His wife nodded glumly. She was more miserable than ever.

But not every change is for the worse. Sometimes a good thing is cut down but grows back even stronger, or two broken halves can make something new, something more complete.

At least that's what the Farmer's Wife and the Landlady decided. And so it was that the hotel was rented out and this provided the wherewithal for a curious arrangement.

The one-time residents of the Flealands Hotel and nearby Cardboard City soon found themselves breathing fresh, country air. They all relocated to Hoggett Hollow! The Landlady took to riding her bike along the country road leading to Hoggett Farm. Nigel and Alan liked to trot along behind her.

Flealick found the pace of country life too slow. Recalling his wild ride clinging to the hospital van, the little dog took to chasing trucks. Hanging on to the mudflap of a roaring delivery van made Flealick's morning.

Inspired by their new, natural setting, the chimpanzees decided to be chimpanzees. Bob, Zootie, Easy and the little twins took up residence in an idyllic patch of rainforest near the Farm.

As for the Orang-utan, he insisted on staying at the farmhouse with Herself. Thelonius would watch Mrs Hoggett's every move as she hung up laundry on the line.

Mrs Hoggett herself took a while to adjust to the Orang-utan's adoring presence. 'Shoo, shoo,' the Farmer's Wife said. But she had found a friend for life.

Sad to say, the thing between the Bull Terrier and the pink poodle didn't last. The poodle ran off with another dog and left him with the kids.

'Ya gotta be scary,' the Bull Terrier urged his pink-haired offspring. 'You're warriors! Now let's hear that snarl!'

The little terrier-poodles whined, 'But, Daaad. Do we have to?'

And finally, Dear Ones, the Pig and the Farmer were content again in each other's company. And things were back to where they started ... more or less.

Farmer Hoggett turned the tap. Deep down in the well, the new pump rumbled into life. Farmer and Pig watched the tap. A gurgle, then a splutter, then a gush of clear water spurted out through the shiny spout!

The Farmer turned to his Pig. 'That'll do, Pig,' he said. 'That'll do.'